Praise for *Toluidine Blue*:

"Imbedded within the fictiona. drama, an interesting and detailed perspective concerning medical forensic examinations relating to criminal acts and the importance to preserve and protect evidence for the judicial process. The reader travels step-by-step from the initial exam to court room proceedings. Stories range from assault, murder, and sexual violation, each demonstrating the value of observing and collecting evidence from the crime scene, the victim, and, when possible, the suspect. Criminal investigators can learn the important contribution of physical forensic examination of injuries and evidence for identifying and connecting a suspect with his/her criminal activity." —Milt Laughland - Retired, FBI Analyst

"As a reader, I like true crime stories, mysteries and thrillers so it's no surprise that I enjoyed *Toluidine Blue*. This is the story of Addie and Rachel, RNs who each become a forensic nurse examiner, or the trained nurse who collects the evidence from victims of sexual assault and other cases. It is compelling, fascinating —and heart-wrenching at the same time—to read about the different cases they work on throughout the book. This is not a book for the faint of heart as it gives the real, gritty description of what victims endure during their assaults. That being said, it serves to educate the reader about the forensics behind sexual assault. Because of language and details of sexual assaults, this is an appropriate read for mature audiences. I would highly recommend it for those who enjoy medical mysteries, true crime stories and suspense novels." —Ellen Gable, award-winning author of nine books

Forensic Nurse Examiners...the search for evidence

...but science can only solve so much....

Toluidine Blue

A Novel

By
Evelyne Margaux Keating
and
Roxanne Shoenfeld

HARD TACK EDITIONS
Baltimore, Maryland

Printed in the United States of America

First edition: February 2019 by Hard Tack Editions, Baltimore, Maryland

ISBN: 9781796904543

Visit: https://toluidineblue.blogspot.com/

Cover design by Thomas Mulgrew III

DEDICATION

To everyone whose heart may be touched by this book.

"There is a longing in our hearts,
For justice, for freedom, for mercy…
For wisdom, for courage,
For comfort...
In weakness, in fear…." —Annc Quigley

TRIGGER WARNING:
This novel contains explicit details of sexual assault and domestic violence. Some of the content may be too disturbing for some readers.

Table of Contents

Introduction

"Fear not, we are of the nature of the lion, and cannot descend to the destruction of mice and such small beasts." —Elizabeth I

Toluidine Blue (pronounced Tol-u-deen) is a novel about forensic nurses and the dedicated care they provide. They pursue justice while striving to heal the emotional wounds of their patients, who are victims of violent sex crimes. Even though names and crime scene locations have been changed, all of the forensic information is accurate, so readers can learn about forensic nursing through the lives of fictional characters. *Toluidine Blue* captures forensic nursing and law enforcement based on elements found in genuine crimes...with added infusions of the criminal justice system.

In the mid-1990's, sexual assault forensic examiners (SAFE nurses) were created, also known as forensic nurse examiners (FNE's), as a group of registered nurses who have had specialized training in order to care for patients who have been sexually assaulted. Over the last two decades forensic nurses have emerged as an elite group. They testify as expert witnesses on sexual assault and forensic evidence collection for the criminal justice system. Forensic nurses are able to teach the jury and the courts about sexual assault and strangulation through the use of State Police Evidence Collection Kits and bodily injuries through the use of body maps and forensic photography.

French criminologist, Dr. Edward Locard (1877-1966) was a pioneer in forensic science, and he is known for the creation of the first police forensic laboratory. Locard's exchange principle states that "every contact leaves a trace." When a person or an object comes in contact with another person or object a transfer of evidence will occur. Forensic nurses look for biological (DNA) and trace evidence that may be transferred during a crime. They also look for injury produced through contact between the victim and the suspect. Prior to the establishment of forensic nurses, only the medical examiner's office collected forensic evidence. Now that there are forensic nurse examiners, you do not have to suffer death in order to receive a forensic exam. Toluidine blue dye is a special solution that adheres only to the cells of injured skin tissue. The dye is absorbed by the deeper cells that become exposed when the skin is broken, thus highlighting the detail of the injury. It is used to enhance the detail in minute bodily injuries to the skin surface. The forensic nurse must understand Locard's exchange principle, in that "a person or object came in contact with another person or object." All injuries big and small are equally significant. Forensic nurses must take the time and effort to closely examine each bodily injury and toluidine blue dye will aid in locating valuable details in the minutest of wounds. Often, it is those details that are enhanced by toluidine blue dye that hold the most valuable physical evidence, bringing truth to the old proverb, "The devil is in the details."

Chapter One: What You Wish For

"Hope is the thing with feathers. That perches in the soul and sings the tune without words and never stops at all." —*Emily Dickinson*

Adeline Donovan had always loved the Baltimore Inner Harbor at night. As the turmoil of the last twelve hours fell away, the air was invigorating against her face. The breeze from the harbor swept over and around her as she sat in the water taxi, watching the lights of Baltimore reflect and dance as on a sea of glass mingled with fire.

"Want one, Miss Addie?" asked the captain of the water taxi.

"Sure, why not? Thank you Cyrus!" She sighed as he lit her cigarette, which for her was indulging in a rare pleasure.

"Hope you ain't cold, Miss Addie," called Cyrus, over the roar of the engines. Cyrus let Addie ride for free ever since she had cared for his granddaughter, who had suffered a gunshot wound to the chest from a stray bullet on Maryland Avenue. In the ER, where Addie worked as a trauma nurse, she had kept the frightened little Zamora calm and reassured, while quickly working on the child, until the trauma team could get her to the operating room. Zamora's worried parents and grandparents had loved Addie for the compassionate care she provided in helping save the child's life.

"I'm good, Cyrus, thanks," Addie replied. "The cold air feels fine after the day I've had. That ER is twelve hours of non-stop controlled chaos."

"We all have days like that, darlin'," said Cyrus. "And you especially in your job. Just relax, honey, and enjoy the view of the harbor."

"Thanks, I will," said Addie. There were not many people on the taxi at that hour, just a few tourists watching the scenery. She closed her eyes for a moment and puffed on her cigarette. Addie had thought her life had been planned out, with all of her dreams coming true. That was gone now, but as Father Fergus had assured her, she was starting anew.

It had been only a day since Addie's world had started falling apart. She had been living with her fiancé, Cain; they had spent the last year planning their wedding. Cain had unassuming good looks. His chiseled jaw complemented his warm, hazel-brown eyes and straight short hair you simply wanted to run your fingers through. He was finishing up law school and Addie was working as a trauma nurse at a city hospital. Addie's job had long caused friction with Cain. Her hours were long; often when she arrived home after a shift she was too exhausted to do anything. She had looked forward to the day she could be a stay-at-home mother and the wife of her soon-to-be successful husband.

She did not know why she had not seen it coming. She had not seen all the cracks in her life until it shattered. Two days ago, on Friday night, Cain and Addie had a dinner to attend with all of the partners of the law firm where he was interning for the summer. He had one year left of law school and hoped that one day he would be a partner at the same prestigious law firm of MacIntyre and Ross. He was excited to finally be invited to join the partners in a social setting, which happened to be at an exclusive address on North Charles Street. He had been talking about it all week, telling Addie, "This is big, really big, I'm just the intern and they have invited me, well, us, to their home for a partners' dinner."

However, on that Friday afternoon Addie had been running late. She remembered trying to explain it to Cain on her cell phone as she drove home. "I'm sorry for being late, babe, but a trauma came in and I couldn't leave. The man was dying."

Cain was curt on the phone. "We're going to be late."

Addie, not wanting to argue, abruptly ended the conversation and turned off her phone before she had an accident behind the wheel. As she drove, she remembered the sight of the man's pale skin and matted, bloodied, stringy, gray hair that was barely attached to the jagged fractured frontal bone. When she walked in the door of their apartment, Cain was pacing and looking at his watch.

She tried to explain. "Cain, I know how important tonight is to you, but the poor man had his skull ripped off the front of his forehead. He was leaning over a hay bailer and leaned too far and got his head in the way of the blade and 'wack' right off with the frontal part of his skull but miraculously, he was alive. I could not leave. My God, Cain, blood was everywhere, I could see his brain! We had to work quickly to get him to surgery. It seemed to be taking forever to get him moved to the operating room. We folded the jagged piece of skull over the exposed, fleshy, pink brain, which looked like pale ribbon candy. You know what I'm talking about? You only see it once a year, at Christmas."

Cain exploded. "Stop it! What the hell is wrong with you, Addie? Normal people don't come home and talk on and on about blood and brains. I don't want to hear about it! We're going to be late. Don't you know how important tonight is? I can't believe you would come in here boasting about how you saved a life."

"But, I'm sorry, I...." Addie was stressed from her day, and upset for letting Cain down.

Cain interrupted her. "You know what? You're always putting your job before us. Don't embarrass me tonight. You know how important this dinner is with the partners. The wives, they'll all be there tonight. Don't talk about all the blood and death of your job — to *anyone.*"

Addie put down her handbag and tried not to lose her temper. "Cain, honey, I'm so sorry I was late. I do know how important tonight's dinner is, but it's also a cocktail party. Actually, we don't have to be there the minute it starts, it's okay to be fashionably late, and arrive a few minutes into the party. I'm sure if I explained why we're late they would understand." Completely exasperated, she rummaged through her jewelry armoire, looking for her rhinestone earrings, opening drawers and slamming them just as briskly. Nearly on the brink of tears, she so wanted Cain to be proud of her.

Cain's voice was taut. "*No.* You are not going to talk about what you do! Those women do not work, they wouldn't understand or care about the blood and violence in the work you do. I don't want you to gross anyone out anyway. Look, we're late, and your job is the reason *why* we're late."

Addie interrupted Cain in a rush of anger, saying, "You can't handle the fact that I, one day, may be equally or, *here*'s a thought ...even *more* successful than you."

12

Cain drove to the party in complete silence. Addie felt sad that Cain was so upset with her, and even sadder that he did not appreciate that she had saved someone's life. She tried to engage in light conversation, but he drove without saying a word. Looking out of the passenger side window, she admired the stately old homes and even older grand trees that surrounded them.

They arrived at a magnificent stone mansion with white pillars surrounding a crescent-shaped porch. Large apple-green ceramic planters of ferns adorned the front entrance along with an elegant *coir* welcome mat. The lady of the house was waiting at the door as they walked up the freshly washed brick walkway. Suddenly, Addie felt one of her Louboutin pumps stick on the bricks so that it was almost yanked off. Dammit, she had stepped on some chewing gum! With a hapless grin on her face she stopped to scrape the shoe against the edge of the brick walk to get rid of the gum. Cain glared at her.

As they entered the house, she felt Cain's fury surround her like an invisible mist. In spite of running late, Addie's glance in the foyer mirror told her that she did not look half-bad. Her blond hair flowed just below her shoulders onto the black fitted dress, adorned by a vintage rhinestone necklace with matching earrings. She glistened in the dim light. Addie ordered a whiskey sour at the catered bar. In Cain's anger, he wrenched open his Heineken with such force that the glass broke, spilling an amber shower of beer all over the Persian carpet. He shot a glance at Addie, making her feel as though it were her fault. She tried to cover her cheshire grin with the rim of her glass as she turned to walk away. It was a marvelous party.

Meandering through the elegant neoclassical house, Addie welcomed thoughts of happier times. She reminisced about when she first met Cain, at an evening outdoor summer party while still in college. Addie's best friend Pam introduced them. Cain had walked over to Addie; both spontaneously smiled at each other. Lanterns hung from the trees softly illuminated their first welcome.

"Well, hello there," he had said. "I get to finally meet you. Pam talked a good bit about you."

Addie could not take her eyes off of him, admiring his muscular arms and chest. "Hello there, to you, too. I'm happy to finally meet you." He stood perfectly straight, his shoulders broad. With his good looks, his defined nose and strong jaw, he reminded her of a warrior. She had known in that moment that he would be part of her forever.

But that was another party, another moment, long ago.

Arriving home after the cocktail party, Addie began to tell Cain of her desire to change career paths and become a forensic nurse. "Cain, remember when I was in college, studying to be a nurse, I loved studying criminal behavior and forensic anthropology. Not only do I have a passion for trauma nursing but also for crime and criminal behavior. I want to change careers. Cain, I want to be a forensic nurse examiner."

But Cain responded with unequivocal vehemence. "No. I don't want a wife with a job that will have you at the beck and call of everyone every time a crime happens. Addie, you just don't understand. You don't get it do you?" Cain retired to his study in stony silence, as Addie cried herself to sleep. Cain was her best friend and she was consumed with love for him. She could never imagine her life without him. She realized the stress he was under, trying to make a life for the two of them. She realized that maybe Cain was right and that working a job that required her to be available any time of the day and night may be unreasonable for their relationship. She decided to redirect her focus in planning for their much anticipated wedding.

The following day was Saturday, and the box of wedding invitations arrived. Addie called out to Cain, who was in his office. "Cain, Cain, the invitations have arrived! They're gorgeous! Closely examining the invitations, she recalled the moment on the beach when he had proposed. He had hidden the ring in her champagne glass. He was afraid she would think there was something in her glass of champagne and throw it across the sand before he could ask her to marry him.

Smiling, she called in the direction of the study, saying, "They turned out exactly how I thought they would." There was no reply. She gazed at the periwinkle lettering on cream stock stationary which read:

Mr. and Mrs. James F. Donovan
cordially invite you to the marriage of their daughter
Adeline Marie
to
Mr. Cain William Pelletier
on September 30th
at 2 o'clock in the afternoon

Cathedral of Mary Our Queen
Baltimore, Maryland.
Reception to follow at The Mansion Castle.

"Only four months away. Wait until you see my dress!" Addie's gown was like none other, strapless, made of white satin with a hint of cream to soften the tone against her fair skin. She whirled around in a circle, as if she had the dress on and was dancing. Still, there was no response from Cain. "The bridesmaids' dresses are ordered, the flowers are ordered, and the reception at the mansion is paid for. Everything is pretty much done and ready for me to walk down the aisle to marry the man that I want to spend the rest of my life with!"

Cain emerged from the office. Addie was so happy, twirling around, laughing, looking at him, adoring his good looks. But he was not smiling. There were tears in his eyes. She paused and took a few steps back.

Cain cleared his throat. "Addie, we need to talk. Finishing law school and getting a job right now is my biggest priority. My family, who have been behind me and helping me through law school, are my second priority. My friends are also my priority. But you, *you* are not my priority. Mainly because I don't seem to be your priority. You're always putting your job first. You can't make a decision without looking at your schedule to see if it interferes with your work. You change your schedule for co-workers but not for us. I don't think this is going to work. I can't marry you. I'm sorry."

Addie was dumbstruck, so stunned she could not even cry. Then her confusion turned to rage. Furiously, she yelled, "How could you do this? How *could* you! The long hours I worked so *you* could finish law school. All of the money my parents and I spent on the wedding, and you, *you* couldn't have figured this out sooner? God damn you!" The couple argued like never before, both feeling as though they had put everything they had into the relationship.

Exhausted, after they raised their voices at each other for what seemed like hours, Addie finally accepted the defeat of their relationship. Slowly, she removed her diamond engagement ring and she put it on the table in front of him. She asked, "I don't even know what part of your body you wash first when you're taking a shower."

Cain placed his right hand over his heart and quietly replied, "Here's where I start, every time." He went back into his office and closed the door. Addie threw the invitations into the kitchen trash can. She poured a glass of wine, and then took a long hot bath, crying and trying to make sense of what had just happened.

Later, Addie hardly remembered anything of that early afternoon, except that she had the presence of mind to call her friend Rachel to come and help her pack. Cain must have showered and gone out, because she did not see him again the rest of the day. Luckily, Rachel, who was also a nurse, was off that Saturday. Rachel and Addie met while working at Trauma One Regional Center, a level one trauma center. Rachel also worked a second job as a death investigator for the State Medical Examiner's office. Addie's mind was spinning; she could hardly see what she was doing. Her hands were shaking; she kept dropping her toiletries. Moving out was the last thing she had planned on doing that weekend.

"You've got to focus, and prioritize one thing at a time. Otherwise, it's too overwhelming." Rachel was carefully folding Addie's clothes and putting them in the suitcase. "Just like you do in the ER. Think of the practical things, such as where you are going to live."

"I have no idea," said Addie, blowing her nose. "Do you know anyone who needs a roommate?"

"Well, you've forgotten that I was looking for a roommate for my apartment down at Fell's Point, in that old cannery building. I have to renew my lease, and a loft apartment is up for rent. It would be perfect for us; it's a two bedroom."

"Oh, Rachel, I have always wanted to live in Fell's Point and in one of those old cannery buildings!"

"You'll love it! And it's right near that bar you like."

"The Whistling Oyster! They have the best whiskey sours! And I love listening to old songs on the jukebox." Addie wiped her face with a Kleenex. "Okay, I'll come by and have a look."

As soon as she was packed, Addie drove to her parents' house in Timonium to tell them her news. Once inside her car, she broke down. She cried so hard; tears flooded her burning cheeks. She hurt so bad inside from the feeling of grief and emptiness. She did not understand why it was over; it just was. Meanwhile, she had left her furniture at Cain's apartment. Her three brothers would move it down to Fell's Point as soon as she could get them all together. She hoped her mother and father would not be too disappointed at the end of her engagement to Cain, not to mention all the money they had already put into the wedding.

She forced herself to think practically about her future. It was hard to put aside her dream of becoming a wife and mother but she needed to move on, and start her own life. Now that Cain was no longer in her life, she could follow her dream. In the fifteen minute drive to her parent's house, Addie had decided to become a forensic nurse examiner.

Addie found her parents enjoying the spring evening by having dinner at the shaded picnic table by the pool in the backyard. Sally Donovan was dishing out some of her delicious homemade potato salad and coleslaw onto vintage rose porcelain plates, along with crispy-edged, Old Bay crab cakes, still steaming from the grill. Her golden blond hair was swept into a French twist accentuating her youthful features. A lavender and white cotton gingham dress, tailored to fit perfectly, flattered her slender figure. "Hi, Addie! You're just in time for dinner!" she exclaimed. Then noticing Addie's eyes full of tears, she gasped. Jim, Addie's father, stood up immediately with concern for his daughter.

"What's happened?" he asked, as she began to sob on his shoulder. Her dad was a handsome Irishman with graying coal black hair and piercing blue eyes. Addie had grown up in a house where there was always activity, relatives coming in and out, and plenty of good food. Her mother managed to create an atmosphere of beauty and simplicity where it was easy to relax and talk. Her mother handed her a glass of iced sweet tea. As she collected herself, she sat in one of the lawn chairs and slowly told her parents what had happened with Cain. They looked at each other helplessly, reflecting each other's stunned pain on her behalf.

"Oh, I am so sorry. What can I do?" asked her mother, hesitantly.

"Would you like a crab cake?" her dad asked.

"Sorry, I can't eat anything now," said Addie, "I'm in such a fog. And I feel bad because of all the money we've spent on the wedding."

"Don't worry about that, honey," Her mother sighed. "Be glad it ended before you walked down the aisle. You're getting off cheap."

"Adeline, we can put your bridal gown in storage. You'll be getting married someday, to someone else," said her dad, trying to be helpful.

"Really, Jim!" Addie's mother shot Dad a look of disapproval, while shaking her head.

"Oh, I can't think about marrying anyone else. I only wanted

Cain. I don't even want to think about my gown or anything to do with weddings."

"Of course you don't, hon." Addie's father fixed a plate of food and set it in front of her.

"Sorry, I'm late!" A deep hearty voice with a thick Irish brogue came from the white trellis gate. It was Father Fergus Magnier, a priest from County Cork who had been their pastor while Addie was growing up. He placed a bottle of wine, Brunello di Montalcino, Addie's favorite, on the table. He was retired now, but often showed up for Saturday supper and conversation at Jim and Sally Donovan's.

"Sit down, Father Ferg! You're just in time," Jim pulled a chair up to the table as Sally loaded yet another plate with potato salad and crab cakes.

"Ah, Miss Addie!" exclaimed Father Ferg. "'Tis been forever and a day since I saw you last."

Addie really did not feel like talking to anyone outside her immediate family but she had to be polite, especially to Father Ferg, who had helped her family through many hard times. She smiled, wanly.

"Addie's wedding has been called off," explained Sally, pouring everyone another round of tea, except for Father Ferg who had his usual pint of Guinness.

"Sorry to hear of that, my dear," said Father Ferg, after blessing the food and drink. "'Tis desperate, desperate indeed! Well, but there is no better remedy for a broken heart than work. Are you still in the nursing profession, Addie?"

"I am, Father. But I am considering going into forensic nursing."

"Now what might that be?" asked Father, as he enjoyed a crab cake. Both her parents raised their heads with expressions of concern and expectation.

"I'll be working with victims of assault, particularly sexual assault, and other violent crimes."

"I guess that means you'll working with police and criminals," mused her dad.

"Something like that. It's something I have wanted to do for a while, but Cain was against it," explained Addie.

"I don't blame him for that," stated her mother. "You could be called out at all hours of the day and night."

"Yes, Mom. But I'll be helping people who need it at the worst time in their life. And it's what I want to do," she said, her voice heavy with conviction.

"As if you don't do enough of that in the emergency room, Addie," Mother said.

"Sounds to me like a brave project; it will be grand," declared Father Ferg. "You'll be performing works of mercy that others shrink from."

Her dad nodded solemnly while her mother rose hastily and went into the kitchen. "She forgot the jello salad," explained Dad. Addie felt uplifted by Father Ferg's words, which confirmed the call she had felt deep in her heart.

"Perhaps we can have a bit of a talk later, my dear. Now, Jim, let's talk politics," said Father Ferg. And the meal continued on a boisterous note.

The next day, Addie visited Rachel at the apartment in Fell's Point. The renovated cannery factory, of only four floors, sat on the water, with a marina attached. Addie toured the two bedroom, fourth floor apartment with a rooftop deck. It seemed to be the perfect start she needed.

"Rachel, I have always wanted to live in Fell's Point and in one of these old cannery buildings. I love it! And to think, we would actually have the fourth floor apartment with vaulted ceilings, and a gorgeous wrought iron spiral staircase leading up to a loft." They walked up the spiral staircase to the loft bedroom. The bedroom was lined with big windows on one side, peeking straight up to the sky, and on the far wall were wooden stairs leading to the deck. "Oh wow! Look it's another staircase leading to a rooftop deck. Oh! This is perfect." From the rooftop deck, the girls could see the Domino's sugar sign and the boats sailing in the Baltimore harbor. "Rach, let's sign the lease." In celebration of their apartment together, they ventured out to the neighborhood bar, The Whistling Oyster. Ordering whiskey sours, with a cherry, they laughed and reminisced while listening to Patsy Cline's "Crazy" playing on the vintage red jukebox in the corner.

That evening, the breeze from the harbor gently caressed her cheeks as she inhaled the fresh air with a sigh. A thousand flickering lights were mirrored around the water taxi as it chugged along. It was time to dream another dream, but this time it would be more than her dream, it would be her reality. She would encounter heaven, she would do battle with hell, fighting on the side of the angels.

Chapter Two: Irony of Death

"It's the decomposition that gets me. You spend your whole life looking after your body. And then you rot away." —Brigitte Bardot

It had been just another typical day in the Emergency Room. Acting charge nurse, Rachel Tristin, was handing-off report to the oncoming charge nurse. It was 7:30 pm on a hot humid Friday night; she knew the seven hour wait would only get worse throughout the night, as soon as the knife and gun clubs came out. Plus she had had another argument with the surgeon, Dr. Emory, who seemed determined to override her authority on every single directive. Exhausted, she sought the restroom, where she brushed out her blonde curls and freshened her make-up. As she left, a tall man in a security guard's uniform held the door of the ER open for her. She had heard that there was a new security guard but she had never seen him up close.

"Thanks!" she said, extending her hand. "I'm Rachel Tristin. Welcome to Emergency." She looked up into his steely eyes in his clean-shaven, light brown face.

"Thank you, Rachel. I'm Jerry. Nice to meet you." He shook her hand, firmly.

"Thank goodness for a gentleman," she thought to herself, and headed to The Whistling Oyster to meet Addie.

At the Oyster, Rachel ran over and hugged Addie, asking "How was your day?" Without waiting for a response Rachel continued. "Mine was horrible. The usual low acuity patients were complaining about wait times and constantly questioning why other patients were being taken to a room before them. Medics lined the hallway with portable monitors beeping constantly. No beds for patients and not enough staff. We had a four-month-old infant brought in by medics in cardiac arrest. We worked so hard on him, but there was nothing more we could do. He was pronounced dead after forty minutes of resuscitation. It was heartbreaking; the mother was crying uncontrollably. She put the baby in bed with her and her boyfriend last night. When mom woke up she realized that she rolled over on the baby in her sleep, and the baby was cold, his lips blue. These cases always affect our staff, especially those with small children of their own."

Addie responded with the shaking of her head with horror. Rachel slowly continued. "As you know, the death of a child has to be reported to the police and to the Medical Examiner's Office. While we were waiting for the Homicide Detectives and the Forensic Investigator to arrive, a cardiac arrest was rolled in by Medic 17. Then a 35-week pregnant patient in active labor came in at the same time. It was a non-stop, very stressful day. Usually, we try to sit down as a group after a critical incident, such as the death of a child, and have a discussion, a debriefing. We had no time to stop and debrief with our staff about the death of the baby. I know several of our staff are going to hug their children tight tonight and not let them go."

Addie nodded. She was exhausted after working as the on-call forensic nurse and began filling Rachel in on her most recent case. "We had another rape victim from the Blair Boulevard corridor. I saw how busy the ER was so I took my patient directly over to the forensics department to do her exam. The ER doc had to come over to me to medically clear her, as there wasn't a room open in the ER. I was wondering how your shift was going, but I had no idea it was that crazy today. I had a hectic day too, but, you know, this is the best job I've ever had. I have no regrets going into forensics. Over the last year, I've already done over fifty cases. We're always busy. "

"There seem to be a lot of those lately, all from Blair Boulevard." Rachel sighed. "I really need a drink. Is that a Knob Creek on the rocks? You're an amazing friend; you always anticipate what I need. I can only have one though; I'm on call for death investigation at midnight."

"Did you see the new security guard at the ER?" asked Addie. "His name is Jerry. I hear he's from Denver."

"I said 'hi' to him before I left, and introduced myself," replied

Rachel. "He's very polite; it's nice to have a gentleman around after dealing with Dr. Emory."

"Oh, man!" exclaimed Addie. "Did you have to deal with *him* again?"

"Did I ever!" Rachel rolled her eyes. "What a jerk! He yelled at me when I suggested having a debriefing for the staff after the death of the baby."

"Oh, no!" Addie exclaimed in disbelief. "You know that they say he is a very good doctor and always puts his patients first."

"I've heard that. I've also heard that he is happily married and that his wife adores him. You'd never know it from the way he acts in the ER when he comes to get his patients to take to the OR for surgery. Don't make him wait!"

"By the way," Addie asked in a lower tone of voice, "did you ever hear from David, your hot firefighter? Sounded like your first date went really well."

"It did," Rachel sighed with disappointment. "But then he seemed to fall off the face of the earth. I tried to call him. I even left messages. Nothing. Not one reply."

Addie and Rachel finished their drinks and went back to their apartment where they sat in their PJs, reminiscing about their friendship, the nursing school years, the mischief they got into, the guys they dated and all the fun they had. Around 11 pm Addie said, "Well, you know what they say, 'the Irish hate to go to bed at night and hate to get up in the morning.' But it's time for me to go to bed."

"Then I don't know what my excuse is," chuckled Rachel. "I'm a good Jewish girl or...*was* until a certain wild Irish rose moved in." They both laughed and went to their rooms.

After a long soak in a hot tub, Rachel fell asleep as soon as her head hit the pillow. Jarringly, her phone rang. Waking up, she looked at the clock; it was 12:30 am. Recognizing the number on her phone, she immediately knew the police dispatcher was calling her. "Hi Rachel, we need you to respond to a deceased male found in Rest Haven Cemetery on the east side of Baltimore."

Rachel asked, "Which area of the cemetery is the body located in?"

The dispatcher responded, "You can't miss him, he's the only dead one above ground."

Rachel rolled her eyes, muttering, "Everybody's a comedian these days." She jumped into a pair of blue jeans, donning a T-shirt that identified her as a Forensic Investigator. She ran her hands through her tangled blonde curls. On her way out she stopped to put on a pair of old, sturdy shoes that she reserved for death investigations then headed out to the scene. As devoted as she was to her job, there were some moments when examining a corpse was the last thing on earth she wanted to do. To pep herself up, she turned on the car radio to that classic rock station she liked. They were playing "There she goes" by The La's. She hummed along. *There she goes, there she goes again....*

Upon arriving at the cemetery it was easy to find the location of the body. The Police Department Crime Lab was there, illuminating an extensive area with powerful lights. The scene was located way in the left rear corner of the cemetery. Rachel noticed several homicide detectives and crime lab techs standing around, waiting for her to arrive and check the pockets of the deceased, hoping to find anything that would identify who he was. Protocol stated that the scene always belonged to the police; however, the body belonged to the medical examiner's office. The police and the crime lab had already taken their scene photographs but they were not supposed to touch the body until the forensic investigator arrived on the scene. It had been over 100 degrees for the past week; according to the display on the car's dashboard it was still 90. That temperature would be recorded on her report. Rachel left the coolness of her car, stepping into the oppressive humidity, a lone drop of sweat made its way down her back, leaving a trail of temporary coolness in its wake.

As she opened her door she was immediately hit with the pungent, familiar odor of a decomposing body. The smell always clung to the hairs of her nostrils, allowing her to smell it when she woke from a deep sleep, even after taking her clothes off at the door, putting them in the washing machine and taking a long, hot shower.

Rachel nodded to homicide Detective Greene with whom she had worked many death investigations over the past nine years. He was a tall, good-looking man with a shaved head and a friendly smile. "And devilishly handsome in a suit," Rachel had often sighed to Addie. Despite the heat, he was wearing a tan suit and looking both handsome and distinguished. She approached him to discuss the case.

"What's the CC number?" asked Rachel, clipboard in hand.

"16-366-0101," replied Detective Greene.

"What time was the case called in?" queried Rachel as she wrote.

"What time was the body found and by whom?"

Detective Greene continued in his most business-like manner. "It was called in by two teenagers whose friends dared them to walk through the cemetery in the dark. Were they in for a surprise! They found the body and immediately called 911 at 11:08 pm. The boys' names are Richard Adler and Dennis Thomas. Here, I wrote their names, addresses, phone numbers and dates of birth on a piece of paper for you."

"Thanks, Detective," she responded, taking the paper from him and studying it in the glare from the bright lights. "Do you have the time of death for me?"

"EMS responded and pronounced him at 11:24 pm; although, we didn't need EMS to tell us this one was dead."

Rachel rolled her eyes. "I guess you're using the address of the cemetery as the location of the call. I assume you are the primary detective for this case?"

Detective Greene grinned. "You know it."

Rachel smiled. "I've already got your number." She documented the details of the case on her clipboard. The information would be used in the report sent to the Office of the Chief Medical Examiner from her computer when she got home. Rachel sensed the tension in the air; everyone wanted to finish the investigation so they could get out of the moist, oppressive heat and back to the coolness of the air conditioning in their cars.

Calmly, Rachel snapped photos of the scene before moving anything, including shots taken from all four corners, walking around the body in a square pattern. The man, lying face up, wore what used to be a crisp white, buttoned-down shirt with the sleeves rolled up. It was now wet with the fluids of decomposition. She looked down at his shoes and, leaning over, noticed the words "Gucci" on the bottoms of them. Donning black latex gloves, she scoured the site for clues to help identify the deceased man lying at her feet, thinking to herself: "A license would be ideal but if I can't find it, then he will go to the medical examiner's office as an 'unknown male.' "

Rachel reached under the body and found a black leather wallet in the back pocket of the man's tailored black dress pants that were saturated with the foul-smelling fluids of decomposition. After photographing the license, Rachel called to Detective Greene: "Hey, I found his driver's license! His name is Carl Givings. He is a white male, lives at 2314 Cross Street and his date of birth is March 24, 1990."

Detective Greene studied the license then said to Rachel: "Due to the advanced stage of decomposition, it's difficult to determine whether the person in the photo on the license is the same person as the guy lying on the ground in front of us."

Nodding in agreement, Rachel replied, "Because of this, I'll send him to the Medical Examiner's Office as an 'unknown male' with a possible ID of the person on the license."

Looking closer at the body, Rachel realized how decomposed he really was. She resumed documenting on her clipboard: "Caucasian male, chunks of facial skin missing."

"He was probably a late-night snack for local animals," proffered Detective Greene.

"After all, protein is protein, and everyone needs to eat," mumbled Rachel, knowing that dark humor was a defense mechanism for most of those who, like herself, had to deal with such grisly situations on a daily basis. Otherwise, they would curl up in a ball and never leave their homes. She coolly continued writing: "Many large fluid-filled blisters noted over the body. Bloating noted over the entire body, blackened areas of skin also identified."   Next, Rachel documented whether rigor mortis was absent, present or passing.

Talking to Detective Greene while examining the body, she stated: "Rigor is the stiffening of the body after death that begins in the smaller muscles of the face and neck, progressing throughout all muscles of the body." Pulling on his forearm, which was bent at a forty-five-degree angle, it straightened without resistance, and remained extended when Rachel let go of it. She quietly told Greene, as she documented that rigor had already passed.

Continuing her exam, Rachel recorded any lividity or livor mortis. The post mortem settling of blood was usually a bluish-purplish color that settled in dependent areas of the body due to gravity. Looking at the pattern of lividity, it was obvious that the man died where he lay and his body had not been moved after death. Rachel noted its location on the body and whether it blanched when she pressed on it. She pressed on the corpse with her gloved covered fingers, noting that it remained bluish-purple in color. "No blanching noted," she added to her clipboard.

Rachel documented the fly eggs in the man's eyes, nose and mouth, feeding on fluid exuded from the body. She recorded that his skin was crawling with small, white maggots, moving in large masses both on and under the skin, some on the ground, moving away from the body. All of Rachel's documentation would assist the medical examiner with determining not only a time of death but also whether the body had been moved post mortem. Detective Greene walked over to Rachel to find out what her observations were.

"He has probably been here for three to five days," she told him. "It's difficult to determine since it has been so hot this week which speeds up the process of decomposition. It's odd that nobody noticed him sooner."

Turning and moving the body, Rachel searched for any injuries on the front and sides of the body. She then rolled the body over to identify any injuries on the back, photographing and documenting as she did so. Next, she helped the Crime Lab Tech take additional photos of the face, body and hands.

As he observed her, Detective Greene asked Rachel, "Do you see any injuries? There appears to be a drop of something that could be dried blood on the tombstone closest to him. Crime lab is taking a sample of it now."

Rachel replied, "I see an area on the back of his skull that appears to be depressed. You know how hard it is to tell when decomposition is this advanced. I guess you'll be at the autopsy in a few hours. No sleep for you." She grimaced at him as she contacted the team who would pick up the body up to come and transport him to the Office of the Chief Medical Examiner. "It's 3:00 am. The autopsy won't be done till around 8:00 am today."

Once the body was picked up, Rachel headed home to write her report. She had to send the report and photos to the Medical Examiner's office before they started morning rounds.

On the way home Rachel's thoughts wandered to David. He had been one of the firefighters who brought a patient in cardiac arrest to the emergency room. He had looked so sexy in his turnout gear; he took her breath away. Rachel sighed as she remembered the sight of his muscular forearms when he was performing CPR. Once the ER staff relieved him from chest compressions, David had glanced up at Rachel. As his eyes caught hers, a wave of magnetism shot between them. He had asked for her phone number, which she quickly wrote down for him, something totally out of character for her. They met for hamburgers at a diner the next day and laughed at each other's silliest jokes. Rachel thought it was the beginning of the romance she had been waiting for all of her life. But he never called after their first date.

It was 3:30 in the morning by the time Rachel arrived at the apartment she rented with Addie. She promptly dropped her clothes that reeked of the stench of rotting flesh into the wash. She took a long, hot shower and settled down with a tall, cold glass of iced tea to begin her report. While writing her report, she mused about the Forensic Nurse Examiner course she would be taking next week. She loved working as a death investigator; however, listening to Addie's stories about her patients had given Rachel the desire to become a forensic nurse. She wanted to help living victims of horrific crimes get through the worst day of their life. She wanted to be instrumental in helping to prevent the people who did such things from hurting anyone else. Knowing that it would be the beginning of a new career for her, Rachel was totally energized about taking the class. She had always been intrigued with anything related to forensics and was excited to be able to build on the knowledge she had from her many years of working as a forensic investigator.

Rachel completed her report, sending both the report and the photographs to the medical examiner's office. She quickly crawled into bed, drifting off to sleep with images of David floating through her subconscious.

A few weeks later, Rachel ran into Detective Greene, "Did you ever determine what happened to the guy in the cemetery?"

Detective Greene replied, brows raised, "We did. We found a receipt from a bar down the street tucked away in his wallet. We also found out that he was a defense attorney. He lived two streets down and seemed to be taking a short cut through the cemetery. He apparently tripped and fell, hitting his head on a tombstone. The cause of death was blunt force trauma to the head. The manner of death was accidental. The irony of death is that it was the headstone of   a   young   girl   who   was   murdered."

Chapter Three: Hack from Hell

"Out of suffering have emerged the strongest souls. The most massive characters are seared with scars."—Khalil Gibran

Addie's cell phone rang on the table next to her bed. It was after midnight and she had just drifted into a really deep sleep. She sat up, grabbing the phone and groggily answered. She was jolted happily awake by the sound of the voice of Detective Frank Knight. "You're needed down at the ER, Addie," said Detective Knight, sounding calm but energetic. "Have you ever heard of a 'hack'?"

"Yes," she responded, her voice soft from slumber. "Someone with a car charges strangers a cheap price for a ride. You know, the people that put out their index finger and shake it up and down while standing on the street. Although, the 'cheap price' might cost them their life. Why? What about it?"

Detective Knight continued. "Sergeant Kate Moran of our Special Victims Unit is with me. She is concerned that Baltimore has serial predators on the loose targeting gay men. We have here the second victim of similar circumstances in a span of ten days. We're in ER room #12."

"I'm on my way."

Addie rose and freshened up, dressing in beige linen slacks, with a black T-shirt, black leather jacket and her most comfortable black high-heel boots. She grabbed her crisp white lab coat as she walked out the door. It was early spring; the evenings were chilly. Getting summoned in the dead of night had become common practice since she started her new career as a forensic nurse. But that was what she had signed up for. She had become better acquainted with the local police detectives, especially Detective Frank Knight, whose professionalism and zeal for solving crimes attracted and inspired her. He was assertive and firm, and did not intimidate easily. Yet he always displayed a kind smile and gentleness towards her. The only problem was that she was distracted by his rugged good looks, blue eyes and muscular build.

Arriving at the hospital, Addie passed Jerry, the security guard, who greeted her warmly as usual. She hoped Dr. Emory was not on duty. Addie approached Detective Frank and Sergeant Kate outside of room #12 in the emergency department, both with serious faces of limited expression. In front of her, Addie pushed a hospital cart containing a police evidence collection kit, including a forensic crime camera. The camera had an alternate light source built into the ring light. She also had two pairs of orange goggles, and a white plastic square on a stand with small holes in it for her to place the swabs she obtained to stand upright, in order to dry before packaging. One pair of orange goggles was for Addie, to identify any fluorescence, and the second pair was for the victim to wear to protect his eyes from the blue glare emitted from the alternate light source.

Frank shook her hand. "Addie! Thanks for coming out. I know it's late." Detective Knight's strong features accentuated his firm jawline and infectious smile.

"It's okay," Addie replied, smiling into his eyes and then turning quickly to face Sergeant Moran. "It must be bad if you're out, Kate."

Kate Moran, a slender, fit woman in her early sixties, with bright hazel eyes and greying, auburn, naturally curly hair, warmly clasped Addie's hand. "Yeah, these guys need to be caught and we're not stopping until they are. Robbing their victims is not what they're really interested in doing. They are monsters who prey on weaker men…men whom they can sexually assault and the victim will not report it."

"Why not?" asked Addie.

"Because they are gay and fear that the police will not believe them. Thankfully, some victims are tough and that, along with your tender care and professionalism, will help us catch those monsters. I'm going to head back to the crime scene. Call Frank with your findings. We'll catch up later." And Kate left.

Addie opened her notebook and turned to Frank. "It's nice to see you. What do we have?"

Frank's expression was grave. "Mr. Todd Meadows. He's a 23-year-old male, trying to get home tonight and caught a ride with two guys in a SUV who held him at gunpoint, beat him, shocked him with a stun gun and sexually assaulted him after tying him up."

Addie nodded as she jotted down his words, trying to maintain a blank expression. "What time did this happen?"

Frank continued. "He got picked up around 10-10:30 pm tonight. A 911 call was placed at 11:30 pm by a woman who found him on the parking lot at the Park-n-Ride at Regency Plaza Blvd. I need you to collect as much evidence as you can. This is possibly the second victim these guys have done this to."

"What's the CC number and what are the charges?" Addie asked. She needed a CC number, the crime control number that the police assigned to this case. Every crime reported received a number.

Frank replied, "The CC number is 77-012-1374 and the suspects, once we catch them, will be charged with physical assault, assault with a deadly weapon, false imprisonment, kidnapping, and sexual assault."

"Thanks," said Addie. "I'll call you with my findings. It'll be a few hours."

"Okay, thanks, and as always, it's nice to see you." Frank smiled as he turned to go. Addie forced herself not to watch him walk away.

Addie took a deep breath and entered the room. Todd Meadows was lying quietly on the stretcher. The ER nurse had been instructed not to clean up the bloodied patient until the forensic nurse arrived to collect evidence and take pictures.

Addie leaned over her patient. "Hi, Todd, my name is Addie. I'm a forensic nurse and I've been called in to take care of you tonight. I'm so sorry about the reason for us meeting, but I'm glad to be here to take care of you. I know you already spoke to detective Knight but, if you can, please tell me what happened."

The small-statured young man with light brown skin, and pale brown eyes appeared much younger than age 23, Addie thought. Plus, he could easily be a model. She could tell he paid meticulous attention to himself, with a buzz cut or "line up" haircut, as it was called in Baltimore, and muscular biceps. She discerned that his smooth skin had been flawless before so many injuries. He was still wearing the bloody clothes from the assault. His pants had once been clean and starched; the starch line was very much present in the dirty pants legs. Blood that had since dried left a dark red linear crust leading from the gash on his forehead down the cheek on his face. His left eye was swollen shut. Quiet and calm, he made one small joke about how bloody he was.

After a few moments of silence, Todd slowly began talking to Addie. "These two guys were going to give me a ride. I told them I only had eight dollars. They seemed pretty cool, so I got in the back. They were asking me all kinds of stuff, like where I work, where I'm from, where do I hang out, just conversation stuff. We were driving for a few minutes when the guy in the passenger's seat, this white dude, he was fat, and his face, he had a big bulbous nose. His skin was all thick and dirty; his hair was dark, long, curly and matted. He pulled out a gun, a solid black gun, and put it to my head and told me they'd kill me if I didn't tell the truth. He started yelling at me, spit was flying out of his mouth, and his forehead was wrinkled, and eyebrows were rising up off his face, he was so angry. It was an instant anger that came out of him. 'I'm gonna asked you again, Where do you live? And you better tell the fuckin' truth. Where do you work? And tell the fuckin' truth, man, or I will blow your fuckin' head off.' He was screaming. I was scared. With the gun pointed in my face, he continued yelling, very demanding, 'You got in the wrong car, tonight ain't gonna be your night! I want your fuckin' coat. Take it off, now! Give me your god damn wallet. Now!' He was yelling, spit was coming out of his mouth from anger, and he was motioning with the gun, pointing it with each movement. I was afraid the gun would just go off. I told the Detectives all of this."

Addie responded as gently as she could. "I need to know the details of the assault, from you, in your own words. I need to know where to collect the best evidence, to link those guys to the crime. Can you describe the driver?"

Todd nodded. "The driver, he's a big black dude, in a black hoodie. His hair was matted, uneven and dirty. No way he's combed his nappy hair in a long time. But I got in, because I didn't want to be judgmental towards them. They did seem nice at first. Until that white guy pulled out his gun, then the driver, he just took off like a bat outta hell. We were on Interstate 695; we shoulda been going towards Blair Heights but he took off to the West side. My heart was racing; I couldn't think, I couldn't put two thoughts together. We were at the Park-n-Ride on the West side near Regency Plaza when he came to a stop so hard we that all jolted forward, you know what I mean? Then we stopped and the guy, the passenger with the gun, he made me get out, that's when it all went bad." His amber eyes welled with tears.

Addie leaned in closer. "You're doing great. Tell me what happened next. What do you mean, it all went bad?"

Todd paused, taking a deep breath. "It all went to hell! The driver, he shocked me in the back, but not one time, it was again and again. The shock made me fall on my knees. I couldn't get up, it was like my muscles were wasted, like rubber bands. I don't know, then they were taking turns beating the shit out of me, with the gun and with their fists and just kicking the crap out of me."

While recounting the assault, he started to cry, hysterically. His tears choked Addie with emotion, but she thought to herself, "I need to be strong for the both of us and to do the job I am here to do...collect forensic evidence to find those fuckers."

Todd went on. "The driver, he grabbed my hands and tied me up, behind my back, when the other dude, laughing, pulled my pants down, down to my ankles. He shocked me again after pulling down my pants. They stank and looked dirty; they smelled like sour, rancid body odor and sweat. They had bad teeth. The white guy said, 'It's hard out here, shit man, you're not sleeping on cardboard!'"

"What else were they saying?"

Todd almost choked in reply. "They were saying stuff like, 'You're my bitch now' and the driver said he was in the military and knows how to break my neck." Todd motioned a head lock. "Then saying 'I have no problem killing you,' holding the gun to my head'."

"What was the look on driver's face?" asked Addie.

Todd replied, "Evil, pure evil, and his eyes were so black. The middle of his eyes were solid black with which made the whites of his seem bright, it was creepy. His brow was furrowed; he looked angry and snarling with his teeth showing."

"Do you remember seeing anything, about his face?"

Todd flinched at the memory. "His nose was really wide and he had gold front teeth. His teeth were bad, nasty and dark yellow."

"Did you tell Detective Knight about this?" queried Addie.

Todd shook his head. "No, I didn't remember it until you asked me. I keep having visions of the assault. It's really weird."

"What can't you forget about tonight?" she asked, softly.

Todd squirmed. "The smell. The smell of my flesh burning, and their dank dirty body smell. But the visions. It's like looking through a photo album but really fast. You know, you see the pictures but not long enough to know what they are. They're just snapshots in your mind, but nothing that I can really remember. But then, I can't forget their smell, and the smell of my burning flesh. Also, his eyes, the blackness in his eyes. I just keep seeing his eyes and those gold front teeth. I'll never forget it."

"The passenger pulled my pants down to my ankles, he was laughing. I was scared, they hated me so bad. I was too scared to cry. I tried to fight back but I couldn't with my hands tied. I couldn't imagine what they were going to do next." He hesitated, crying and embarrassed to tell what happened next. He slowly described in detail more of the sexual torture inflicted upon him by the perpetrators. Addie cringed inside as she struggled against an overwhelming feeling of revulsion. Todd sobbed for a few moments and then went on.

"He kneed me in my chest, really hard, moving my body by force. My knees moved on the sharp gravel and tiny pointed pebbles, I could feel the gravel cutting my knees. Shortly after forcing me down onto the hard, sharp gravel, I could feel the warmth of my blood pouring out of the gashes created by the pebbles cutting deep into my skin. The driver was taking pictures of me, naked from the waist down with my pants at my ankles, my face and knees bleeding and my hands tied behind my back with a cord, he took pictures of the whole thing. Then, while still on my knees, he hit me in the right side of my head, with his left fist, I hit the ground on my left side, the gravel embedded in my skin. I lay there motionless. I wanted them to think they killed me. Part of me wished they had."

There was blood on Todd's face from the deep jagged laceration to his forehead caused by the blunt force trauma from the gun being bashed into the forehead. His floral tee shirt and chino pants were covered in blood.

"I'm sorry you had to go through this." Addie placed her hand reassuringly on Todd's shoulder. "I know the police will work tirelessly until they find those guys." She halted a moment. "I need you to sign a consent form for forensic examination and evidence collection. This consent form allows me to perform a head-to-toe exam, obtain a forensic history and medical history, take photographs of injuries and of your genitals as well. I will need to collect all of your clothing. You may refuse any part of the exam, at any time. Todd, I will move through the exam at a pace that is most comfortable for you. Do you have any questions?"

Tears streamed down Todd's face. "No. I can't believe this has happened. I didn't think they would do this to me. Why? If they wanted to rob me, they should have just done it, but I told them, I only had eight dollars. But to assault me and humiliate me like that. I, I just can't believe it."

Addie forged ahead as calmly as possible. "Let's start with your facial injuries. What were you hit with? You have a huge gash in your forehead and a very swollen eye. I'll get facial x-rays to make sure nothing is broken, and the emergency room doctor will need to put some stitches in your forehead, but meanwhile, tell me again what happened to your face?"

Todd replied, "I told the Detective, what is his name, Knight? They had a handgun; it was black. The passenger hit me over and over again in the head and forehead, so much that I got dizzy and I think I blacked out, but I don't remember."

Addie filled out a photo documentation page, writing with a black Sharpie:

PHOTO DOCUMENTATION
CC#: 77-012-1274
VICTIM: Todd Meadows
DETECTIVE: Frank Knight/ Sgt. Kate Moran
FNE: Addie Donovan, BSN, RN FNE- A/P, SANE
CHARGES: 1ST DEGREE SEX ASSAULT, FALSE IMPRISONMENT, KIDNAPPING, 1ST DEGREE PHYSICAL ASSAULT

Addie took photographs of Todd, starting with the entire body, while he was still wearing the clothes that he was assaulted in, photo documenting his bloody clothing and his pants which were torn open from the front. Next, she took a photo of his face from a few feet away, not to show the injuries but to capture a photo of him, as a person, at the moment, after enduring the assault.

Addie examined the injuries to his forehead and nose. She examined the inside of Todd's mouth for injury, finding purple and blue bruises to his lower front lip. "I am going to swab the inside of your cheeks on both sides." Addie used one swab for each side of the cheek, rolling it on the inside of the cheek for collection of the buccal swabs, saying: "This is so the police have a known DNA from you to compare to any DNA that might be recovered from the scene." Then Addie placed the swabs in the holes of the swab drying tray, keeping the swabs upright to dry. "Next, I need to take photographs of the burn marks to the outside of your shirt and then I need you to take off your shirt for evidence. When you hand it to me please don't let it fall on the floor."

Addie placed the shirt in a brown paper bag labeled "evidence" and wrote the information on the bag. She filled out the label already fixed on the paper bag with the crime control number, the victim's name, the forensic examiner's name, and the date/time. Such data was important in order to maintain the chain of custody. Lastly, she sealed the bag with a strip of blue police evidence tape, signing her name across the tape with the CC number, date and time. She then collected his pants and underwear and placed them in separate paper bags, repeating the same steps as with the shirt. Addie noticed dried dark blood in the underwear.

Todd was talking as Addie collected his clothing. "I really don't really know what happened to my face. The guy with the gun, he started whipping me in the face with it, really hard. I could hear it, you know, the gun hitting my forehead. It sounded like a dense thud. When he stopped, the driver came over and started punching me in the face, over and over again. They were saying things to each other, but I don't know what they were saying. They sounded angry, with a malicious tone in their voices. I couldn't comprehend anything that they were saying. I felt nothing except for confusion, and then I blacked out."

Experience made it easier to ask the difficult questions. "Were you standing or were you on the ground when they were beating you?" asked Addie.

"I was on the ground, in the parking lot, where they made me get out of the van. I can taste the dirt and feel the grit on my tongue and the roof of my mouth."

Addie noticed sand, dirt and small stones from asphalt in his hair and faint abrasions on his neck and face. His clothing also had dirt stains, as well as faint signs of wear in the material from the friction of his body moving on the asphalt when he was being assaulted. She could smell the asphalt and dirt, but it was not the fresh smell of gardening dirt. It was more of an offensive, gasoline, putrid smell that permeates your nostrils.

After a few moments, Addie said, "Okay. I'm going to take a series of photographs of the injuries to your face." She started taking forensic photos to include with her report for the police. She took intermediate photos of all of Todd's facial injuries from about one to two feet. She concluded with multiple photos of each individual injury on his face, using a ruler for accurate measurement of the size of each laceration caused by the blunt force trauma from the gun and their fists. Photographing his face took a lot of time, but it was crucial to document each aspect of the crime. The purple and blue bruises and swelling on his head were easily concealed by his short hair and so required more time. Addie started with the top of Todd's head and methodically worked her way down. Next, she focused her attention on the large gaping laceration to his forehead, photographing and documenting the laceration on her body map.

Addie placed a blue drape towel under Todd's head to photograph the laceration to the forehead. The blue drape provided an 18% gray color required to capture color accuracy of injuries in forensic photography. One photograph was of the injury, while a second photograph documented the exact size with a ruler. The ruler accurately measured the jagged laceration. She took additional photos of his deformed, swollen nose and painful, blue-bruised, swollen eyes. The usually white scleras of his eyes were speckled in red petechial dots from crying and possibly from suffocation. The oral obstruction from a filthy penis forced in his throat had suffocated Todd while he was on his knees. She said to Todd, "I am going to continue my assessment and examine your neck, chest and back. Does anything hurt in these areas?"

"Yeah, an area on my back burns," Todd replied. "I felt a 'shock' in my back, which really hurt and made my legs give way. I couldn't stand up."

"When did you feel this 'shock' sensation?"

Todd answered. "At the parking lot, as soon as I got out of the van, the driver came around and I think he had a taser or stun gun and I felt a hot, burning sensation on my back."

Addie examined his back. "There are several sets of two burn marks; they seem to be linked with a welt on your back. Is it here you have the pain?"

Todd gasped. "Ah, yes! That hurts, what are you doing?"

"I'm sorry, Todd. I'm going to take a few photographs of the burns." Addie took a series of three photos: orientation, intermediate, and close up photographs. She snapped a few more photos using a gray scale ruler to measure the burns, the grey scale documenting accurate lighting and ensuring a ninety degree angle for the photographs as well, to prove in court that they are a fair and accurate representation of what she examined. Meanwhile, she continued to document all of his injuries on a body map.

"What do you see?" inquired Todd. "Can you see where I was shocked?"

"If you could sit up again please," asked Addie, and she closely examined his back. "Yeah, looks like a typical stun gun injury, two small burn marks with a red, raised welt linking them together. I can see you were shocked with the stun gun several times. This pattern of burns is found in several places on your back. I am going to apply a blue dye, called toluidine, that will help me visualize your injuries and help the burns show up on photographs as well. The blue dye will also determine whether this pattern of injury is new or normal skin variation for you. It confirms that this is a fresh injury and happened tonight. So no defense lawyer can say it's a normal skin discoloration. Basically, it will help us in court."

Todd, whose eyes widened, as his eyebrows rose in surprise, exclaimed, "Court! I have to go to court? I can't do that! I don't want to see these guys ever again." Shaking his head back and forth, "I will never get that guy's face out of my mind! I never want to see them again! That one, with the black eyes, he is evil, pure evil."

Addie placed her hand on Todd's shoulders, reassuring him. "It's okay. It's going to be okay. Let's just get through tonight. We don't have to worry about anything else right now. I will also be in court to testify to my findings. But, let's just focus on the 'right now' and get through tonight." She felt him shudder. "I am sorry for the circumstances but I am glad to be here for you." She went on, her mouth dry. "I have to collect as many photos and as much evidence as I can in order to help you and get those guys caught. They will continue kidnapping and assaulting people until they get put away, permanently! You're doing great, Todd. Just a few more questions and a bit more evidence to collect and then I'm finished. But when I'm finished, I'll call in a victim advocate to help you navigate through the next steps." Todd nodded. "Now, I need to examine your knees. My God, they look painful."

Both of Todd's knees were red, swollen with abrasions to the surface and deep jagged lacerations in the center of the abrasions. Small pieces of dirt were embedded in the deep lacerations; she noted dried blood from his knees to his ankles. "My last series of photos will be of your knees, so maybe six more photos and I will be finished your exam." Using a forensic ruler Addie measured the injuries to Todd's knees. The abrasions measured seven centimeters, linear laceration to the left knee and two five centimeter lacerations across the right knee. "Since they have your home address, we need to find someplace for you to stay. Can you stay with family until the apartment management finds another apartment for you to move to?"

"I have family here," Todd told her. "So I can stay with my mom. They have my address. Do you think they will go to my apartment?"

Addie placed her hand on his shoulder again. "Not to get sidetracked from your exam, but let's finish, and then I'll let Ms. Valerie Kelly, our victim advocate, know that you need a new place to live, she will help you with that." Examining his wrists, Addie noted ligature marks have made a furrowing in the skin, circumferential around both of his wrists. The furrowing was deep and had broken the skin, causing an abrasion. The abrasions, although shearing the skin's surface, were not deep enough to bleed.

"Are your wrists painful?

"Yeah, they're pretty tender."

"I would like to put some of the dye that I used before, the toluidine blue dye, to help enhance the area of the skin that's injured. It's tough for me to see if there are multiple ligature marks or just one and if the other lines are just normal creases in your skin. The dye will only adhere to broken skin so it is really helpful to determine the extent of the injuries. Toluidine dye also confirms if an injury is acute, meaning, that the injury happened within the last several hours, before the skin has had time to heal."

Multiple abrasions made by the ligature were visible. The injured tissue had turned blue after the dye was gently removed. "Now I can clearly see that they had tied the ligature around both of your wrists several times" murmured Addie. "I need to finish taking photographs of the ligature marks, especially now that I can see them more clearly. Do you know what you were tied up with?"

Todd sighed. "Yeah, they are pretty painful. They used a blue cord to tie my hands behind my back, but I don't know how many times they wrapped the cord around. My hands were behind my back, so I had no way of knowing." His tears slid down his cheeks.

Addie spoke calmly. "If you would lie on your stomach, I need to examine your anal area. Are you having a lot of pain?"

Todd, rolling over slowly and grimacing in pain from the movement, muttered, "It hurt really bad. Are you going to make it hurt again? I can hardly sit down. The one guy, he kept stabbing and prodding me in my ass with something. I don't know what they forced in me, but it was really painful. Is this going to hurt? Why do you have to do this?"

Addie examined his back and buttocks. "I hope not to hurt you, but it is important that I examine you carefully for any injury." She documented on the body map the debris, ranging from dirt to small pebbles on his buttocks. For Addie, the debris confirmed that his pants were pulled down and his genitals and anus were exposed, as he had reported.

She said, "Since you're not sure what happened, and you're having pain in this area, I need to look for any small tears or lacerations." She found debris on his genitals, buttocks and in his anal opening. She gently rolled a wet swab and then rolled a dry swab collecting a sample of the debris, also hoping for DNA. Addie examined his anal opening looking for small tears, but the tears were difficult to identify from the normal wrinkles surrounding the anal opening. Addie removed a sterile swab from the paper sheath, very carefully pressed around the anus. Todd was startled from the pain. "Oh, that's really sore!"

Concerned that an injury might be missed, Addie placed the toluidine blue dye on a sterile swab and applied the dye around the anal opening. Tears were confirmed at the 9 o'clock and 11 o'clock positions around the anal opening by the uptake of blue dye. The anal tears were forensically photographed as evidence of sodomy from fingers or an object he reported "being prodded with."

"Todd, I'm all finished," said Addie gently. "You can sit up now."

Todd carefully turned over, grimacing in pain from each movement. "My entire body hurts." He started crying again, this time shuddering with big tears streaming down his face.

Addie sat down on an exam stool, looking at him. Tilting her head slightly to the side and softening her eyes, she said. "Todd, you did great during the exam. I know you have faced a nightmare, and then to have to come in here, with me, swabbing your body and asking you details having you relive the event, is really difficult. But you are very strong to go through with the exam. While you are here in the ER, I want to get the results of the x-rays of your face and of the EKG, especially after being shocked so many times."

Todd's eyes widened and filled with tears. But he said nothing.

Addie went on. "Since I collected your clothes, let's pick out a new shirt and pants for you to go home in." Addie pulled open two large cabinet doors. Inside were double shelves, full of donated clothing in all sizes for children, women, and men to wear after their clothes had been collected as evidence after a sexual assault. "How about a brown shirt? Long sleeves?" Addie held it up to see if it fit him.

"Nope, too boxy for me."

Addie pulled out another. "How about...oh, never mind, this is horrible." She turned the sweatshirt around, showing the shirt to Todd. It was a navy blue sweatshirt with a black and white tuxedo cat with rainbow colored bow tie eating an ice cream cone, with "Purrfectly Delicious" in hot pink lettering. Angrily, she exclaimed, "Who the hell would donate this to a sexual assault unit?"

Todd looked at the sweatshirt and while reading it, burst into laughter. Uncontrollable laughter from both of them filled the room. It was the exact stupid humor they both needed to ease the stress.

"Okay, here's a nice dress shirt, and I have new tan chinos for you, and they still have the tags on them. How about this?"

Todd smiled. "I like it." Suddenly, the reality of why they were picking out a new outfit soon came back, with a somber air penetrating the room. Todd started crying again. Sitting on the stretcher, his face in his hands, he wept. He was crying so hard that his shoulders shook uncontrollably. Addie's eyes brimmed with tears; she averted her gaze, shaking her head, in total disbelief of how one human being can torture another so brutally. She knew she would carry the burden of this case for some time, perhaps forever. Both of their emotions ranging from laughter to tears made the situation real, with Addie aware that there never is a typical sexual assault response but the vehement swinging of emotions.

Addie, blinking her tears away, enthusiastically introduced the victim advocate, Valerie Kelly. Valerie was very attractive with soft blue eyes and dark brown hair, freshly curled after a Saturday evening out with her boyfriend. She was as compassionate as she was pretty. "This is Ms. Kelly, she prefers 'Val'. She's the wonderful advocate that I've called in to help and she will assist in the next step. Val will provide counseling services and locate a safe place for you to live. I know it's a tough exam, but you did a great job. The detectives will be in touch in the next day or two. If you remember anything else, you need to let them know. Details often come to memory after sleeping and giving yourself time to process what has happened tonight." Todd extended his arms to give Addie a hug of appreciation.

"Hi, Mr. Meadows, I'm Val. I would like us to go into an interview room, down the hall, so we can talk. There is a sofa in there, so you might be a little more comfortable." Todd walked away, talking to Val.

Addie called Detective Knight on his cell phone. "Hi, are you still awake?"

Frank replied, "Yup, I was waiting for you to call. I went back to the parking lot and met up with Sergeant Moran. We were curious to see if there are any security cameras or if there was anything we missed the first time we were there. What did you find out? Did he disclose anything else to you?"

"His story is the same as what you told me," responded Addie. "He's pretty consistent. He has no idea who they are. The laceration to his forehead is five centimeters in length and required eight sutures by the emergency room doc. The forehead lac, according to Mr. Meadows, was from being pistol whipped. I had X-rays of his nose done; the ER doc told me that he has a nasal fracture. I found several sets of burn pattern consistent with a two prong stun gun that made direct contact with his back at least four times. I photographed all of the injuries to his face, the burns, the anal tears and the ligature marks to both his wrists. I could see that the ligature was wrapped around both of his wrists three times, so these guys were serious about tying him up. Did the responding officer cut the ligature off on the opposite side of the knot? I sure hope they preserved the knot to compare it to the patient that our new forensic nurse, Lisa, did last week. Have you met her yet? She is really good and will be a huge asset to our team."

"Yeah, I did meet Lisa, her report was good," Frank replied. "Ashley, your other cohort in crime, was training her. The crime lab preserved the knot and submitted it from the case last week, also a gay male victim."

"Sounds like the same guys, same MO—gay male, kidnapped at gunpoint after hacking a ride, overcome with a stun gun, anally assaulted, and beaten with the gun. They did a number on this guy. He's really lucky they didn't kill him. But, their next victim might not be so lucky. Do you think it's the same guys from the case last week?"

"Yes, I do," asserted Frank. "There are too many similarities."

"Do you think those guys are also raping woman on Blair Boulevard?"

"Now, that's a problem. No, the *modus operandi* is different. I think we have these two guys maliciously attacking gay men and a separate serial rapist stalking and violently attacking women. Their MO's are completely different."

"So you think those guys, they're preying only on gay men?" mused Addie. "Oh, I almost forgot to tell you, he mentioned that the driver had a wide nose and two gold front teeth and he smoked Kool cigarettes. Todd talked a lot and it's all in my report."

"Okay, sounds good. According to Sergeant Moran, they like to talk to you ladies because you are their security at a time where life or humanity let them down. When we first talk to these victims, they are still traumatized and many victims think they told the police everything that has happened to them. My fellow detectives and I appreciate that when you and your team of forensic nurses realize that the victim just told you something really important to the case during the exam, and you contact us immediately. Most of the time we're still at the crime scene. The bottom line is, I hate when they tell you guys stuff that they don't tell us. I'll make sure the crime lab looks for Kool cigarette butts at the crime scene. We'll go back to the crime scene after daybreak. It was too dark when we went back last night to see anything. I'll be sure to let patrol know that one of the suspects is really ugly with a big nose and crazy gold front teeth." Frank paused a moment and Addie wondered if he had that faint glimmer of a smile that she found so mysterious. "The two cases, both being gay men, are similar and I'm pretty sure that they're connected. But I agree, the comparison of the knots used will be helpful. Addie, we have to find these guys, they're going to kill their next victim, I know it. Thanks a lot for your help tonight. As always, I appreciate it. Be safe driving home. God, I can't believe it's going on 4 am already. Good night."

"My night's not over yet," replied Addie. "I still have to write up my report and package the evidence and call for the crime lab to come and pick it up. I'll be here for another three hours or more. I'll have your copy of the report ready when the crime lab comes. It will be in a marked confidential large manila envelope. You'll have your report by tomorrow."

Frank interrupted her. "Why don't you hold the copy of my report? I'll meet you in your office on, say Monday, and we can go over it together. That way if I have any questions, you know, you can clear it up for me."

"Yeah, I'll be in on Monday, that's fine. It will give me extra time to up load the photos and to review the chart again. I'm so tired right now. I'll see you Monday."

Chapter 4: Trust Is Where Peace Flows

"Now that you know the truth of who you really are, go and live your life fearlessly!" —Anita Moorjani

On Monday morning, they started their day as if it was any other day. Addie and Rachel sat on the sofa in the living room, enjoying the warmth in their loft apartment. While savoring their morning coffee, they watched the weather on the late morning news. "Happy April Fools' Day, but snow is no April Fools'," declared the reporter. "Today will be in the upper 20's with slight winds from the North. Ice and sleet Monday morning, turning to snow by 11am. More details to follow."

Addie, with hair in curlers, turned to Rachel, "Why do they always do that?"

"Do what?" Rachel yawned, giving Addie a perplexed look.

"The news," she replied with a chuckle. "They tell you 'details to follow' to hear about the really bad weather that may impact your day. Or you have to wait...'coming up next' to find out what 'everyday household item might kill you.' It drives me crazy."

Rachel covered her mouth as she laughed out loud, "You're so right, they always do that!" she sipped her coffee. "April 1 and calling for snow? Oh, it's 10:00 am already! I have to get off this sofa to get ready for a meeting at the medical examiner's office. I'll stay downtown today, so I don't really care about the weather."

Addie, still planted in her cozy spot, wrapped in a faux fur blanket, at the opposite end of their cognac leather sofa, "I need to get ready for work, too. I have to meet Frank today at 10:45 am, and I don't want to be late. He wants to go over my case from Saturday." She stood up from the sofa. "Although, I don't know why he can't read my forensic report like the rest of the detectives."

"Maybe he just wants to be with you," speculated Rachel, with a wink. "You had better look your best."

"Well, I'll dress warmly. I guess I'll have to take my chances on the weather." Addie's voice was calm and nonchalant although her heart fluttered.

The home phone in the kitchen rang. Addie's nurse manager was calling to cancel the statewide violent crimes meeting. "Hey, it's Laura. Several members of the council can't make it to the meeting today, so I've decided to cancel. I'll be working from home today because of the ice and snow."

Addie replied, "Okay. I'm going in to the office to meet Detective Knight to go over my report from our case on Saturday. I'll probably stay a few hours to get caught up. I want to upload the photos, and look over Mr. Meadow's injuries again, make sure I didn't miss anything. Enjoy your snow day!"

"Sounds good. I'll be in tomorrow, so I'll see you then. I can't wait to see the pictures. I read your report yesterday. How brutal!"

"Yeah, he suffered a lot of injuries. Val talked to him, she's so supportive. I hope he follows up with counseling. He's going to need help recovering emotionally. I'll see you tomorrow, and I will update you on today's meeting with Detective Knight."

"Okay, thanks. Bye."

Addie hung up the phone and walked back into the dining room to continue her conversation with Rachel. But Rachel was heading to her room.

"I think Frank has a thing for you," Rachel said, bluntly, pausing in the doorway.

Addie blushed. "Well, we talk on the phone or text almost every day. We always seem to sit together in meetings. We all go out, you know, the nurses and detectives, well, we all went out a few times and Frank and I always spend the entire time talking or sitting together. I just don't know if I should mix my personal life with my professional one, that's all. But for now, I think we both sense some pretty strong feelings." Raising her eyebrows, she smiled to herself.

"Just see how it goes." Rachel called from her room. "I can't wait to see who will cave first."

Addie finished her coffee. Grinning, she ran up the ornate black metal spiral staircase that separated their living and dining room, to finish getting ready for work. The front door of their grand loft apartment opened into the dining room, in which the ceiling was thirty feet high. Addie's bedroom was in the loft over the living room, since the living room ceiling was only ten feet tall, it made Addie's bedroom quite cozy. Windows lined the entire back brick wall of the old cannery, the living room windows extended up to the ceiling of the second floor loft bedroom, bright and airy.

Addie's pastel blue angora sweater was the warmest top she owned. Plus, she wondered if Frank might notice her in the soft sweater. She also decided to wear her tailored black wool dress pants, hoping they will keep her nice and warm, too. She had done her makeup earlier in the morning, so it only took her a few minutes to finish getting dressed for work. She left her loft bedroom and went back down the metal wrought iron staircase.

The pale blue sweater softened her black wool winter coat, with only the angora turtleneck showing beneath. As she buttoned her coat, she simultaneously slid her right foot into a black and white zebra-striped clog. Buttoning the last button on her coat, she slid her left foot into her other zebra-striped clog. Although she preferred high-heeled black leather boots over clogs, she thought she did not want to slip on the ice and break her neck.

With one last glance in the mirror, she checked to see if her shimmering pink lipstick had smudged while putting on her coat. She smacked her lips together to ensure her glossy lipstick was even. Addie, while putting on her rose-gold hoop earrings, called, "Rachel, I'm leaving! I'll see you tonight. Maybe we can go out to dinner, just you, me and Kate? We can walk down to The Whistling Oyster if it snows. I wish I knew the forecast for today, aside from 'chance of snow, coming up next…details to follow.' Hopefully Kate can go out, too. I don't think many people realize you, me and Sergeant Moran live in the same building! But, she likes to keep her personal life just that, personal."

"Have a good day, Addie! Dinner sounds great! See you tonight!" Rachel called from the short hallway running parallel to her first floor bedroom.

Addie knew she needed quick access to her badge, in order to gain entry into the forensics department in the hospital, so she put her ID badge on last. She carefully looped it over her head, trying not to mess up her hair or make-up, the black-colored lanyard with FORENSIC NURSE in white-stamped lettering, and attached was her hospital badge. Under her picture it read:

Addie, BSN, RN, FNE A/P, SANE
Forensic Nurse Examiner.

Addie's team of forensic nurses had their last names purposely left off their hospital ID's. Not disclosing their last names was an attempt by the hospital to protect the nurses from retaliation that might come primarily from suspects. The job of a forensic nurse was also to collect evidence from suspects, for comparison to any evidence found at rape scenes. Whatever the search warrant read was what the forensic nurse would collect. The detectives either brought the suspect to the emergency room for the suspect exam, or the forensic nurse would travel to the jail. The forensic nurse went inside the jail to collect evidence from violent suspects, who posed too great a threat to the emergency room. The nurses always entered the jail with police escort to ensure their own safety. Addie hoped she did not get any search warrants that would need to be executed on the potentially icy, snowy day.

Even her warmest outfit still could not protect her from the brisk sleet. The old canning factory faced the harbor in Fell's Point; the parking lot was bordered on two sides by a marina. Being on the water, the wind was strong and cold. Addie could not wait to get into her car; she could see her beloved white Audi A-4 across the parking lot. As she walked briskly, she squinted her eyes to keep the tiny ice pellets away, but her eyes started to get irritated and began to water. So she jogged across the parking lot to her car, with her head down, protecting her eyes and face, and her coat held up around her neck, attempting to keep away the stabbing cold.

As soon as Addie got into her car, she locked the doors, as she always did. Sitting waiting for the car to warm up, she glanced over the few boats left in the marina over the winter, "Maybe they're waiting for a warm day to go on a sail?" Grandma and Pop lived in a grand Tudor-revival house in Scarsdale, NY. Addie remembered sailing with her grandfather as a child on Long Island Sound, along with her dad and brothers. They always enjoyed spending an afternoon sailing with Pop, out on the *Hard Tack*. The sailboat was thirty feet long, which seemed enormous to me. Pop proudly purchased the *Hard Tack* in the 1960's, with a fiberglass haul, crisp white sail, and beautiful hand rubbed mahogany wood trim; it was truly reminiscent of an era of craftsmanship. Grandma and Mom never sailed, but would have a wonderful dinner prepared when the hungry bunch returned from their maritime adventure. "Mom still makes the best homemade pies," she said aloud to herself

Rubbing her hands together, she spied her black leather gloves on the passenger side floor. The warm air was starting to blow from the vents, removing the shaking chill from her body. She put on the leather gloves, but winced from the cold inside them. Within minutes, the leather gloves warmed her red hands.

The city roads were not too slushy but the rural county roads were quite different. While driving on a four lane county road, with the safety of a center turn lane, Addie cautiously poked along at 20 miles per hour due to the ice and sleet. Running late for work because of the slick road conditions, she exclaimed to herself, "Dammit! Why can't the news warn you of the road conditions? I bet this was what they meant - 'details to follow.' I'm going to be late meeting Frank."

Stopping at a red light, Addie dug through her purse with her right hand while keeping close watch on the car in front of her. She pulled out her cell phone; the phone battery was at fifteen percent. Looking at the nearly dead phone she realized, "Oh, my God. I forgot to charge my phone. No!" She tilted her head back, exasperated, and after taking in a deep sigh, she thought, "Maybe I can make one last phone call before my phone dies." She brought up Frank in her contacts and the phone dialed, quickly going to voicemail. Not wanting to waste her battery, she quickly disconnected the call. As the light changed green, Addie threw the cell phone back into her purse. Focusing more on the road, and not on her phone or how late she was, she tried to enjoy the resplendence of the wintry morning.

Turning on the radio, she heard the DJ announce: "An unexpected spring nor'easter has headed up the East Coast bringing three to five inches of snow today and eight to twelve inches tonight. We are currently under a winter weather watch until 8 pm, when it will turn into a Winter Weather Advisory."

"What?" Addie thought. "It was 67 degrees over the weekend! Where did this storm come from? 'Baltimore weather, if you don't like it, wait a few days.' Now the roads are horrible. It's too bad the meeting was cancelled, but now I know why. The meetings are usually pretty interesting, plus I always enjoy hearing what crimes and issues are at the top of the list of Sergeant Kate Moran; especially her updates on cold case hits in Maryland. I like to see my favorites from the state's attorney's office, my favorite detectives and of course my other forensic nurses, Laura, Ashley, Bobbi and Lisa. It's seldom we're all together. I can't imagine how bad the roads will be by 2:00 pm. Oh, it's 11:00 am already. I was supposed to meet Frank fifteen minutes ago. I can't believe I forgot to charge my phone this morning."

Addie peered up at the sky, which had changed from sleet to snow. Big wet snowflakes were hitting the windshield. The snowflakes were so big they were falling like stars, mingling the natural with the magical. They were now coating the grass and the roads. The roads were treacherous and slippery from accumulating ice and slush. The radio was playing "My Idea of Heaven" by Leigh Nash. She lost herself in her thoughts, finding the snowflakes addicting to watch, but they kept taking her attention off the road. Further reducing her attention—was hunger. "God, I'm hungry; I hope I have time to grab something quick at 7-11. But I know Frank is waiting for me to go over the report from Todd's case. Hopefully, it will only take me another 30 minutes to get to work. I am never late for anything. I'm sure he won't mind me being late this once."

Brake lights were shining on the wet road, creating a steady glow of red light. Addie noticed a short yellow bus and beyond the bus, a white pickup truck in the median. As she approached, she focused her full attention on the slowing traffic, fearing what might lie ahead.

"Nooo, please, nooo," she groaned to herself. "Oh, I hope the school bus wasn't in an accident. But with everyone driving by and no one stopping, the bus couldn't have been involved, others would have stopped, I'm sure. Maybe the school bus just broke down."

As Addie moved a little closer, she observed debris all over the two oncoming lanes, stopping on-coming traffic on the other side of the road. Still hoping the handicapped children's yellow school bus was not involved, Addie put her window down to get a better view as she drove by. The snow had caused her driver's side window to be blurry. The cold air hit her hard in the face, along with a few fat wet snow flakes, "Oh! It's cold!" Turning up the heat in her car to deter the freezing cold air from coming in, she continued driving slowly, driving only about 5 miles an hour. The traffic crawled. The road was slushy, with icy crystals about an inch deep and very slippery. She was very careful not to slide and hit something. As she approached the school bus, rolling her window down, she heard children crying.

Addie felt the frightening cries from the children like a hand squeezing her heart. She blinked her tears back, while looking for a safe place to pull over to help. The traffic was driving slowly in front and behind her, two lanes thick. She had no choice but to continue by the bus and white pickup truck. Driving by the bus, she noticed the driver's side was crumpled inward. The driver's window was smashed with the tempered glass square pieces scattered all over the street. The side of the bus, where the children would be seated, was pushed in toward the children's seats. Shattered glass windows on the side of the bus were still in one piece, but spider-webbed. However, one large piece of shattered tempered glass had unsteadily caved in toward the children, leaning inside of the bus, ready to cave in at any moment. She saw movement of people on the bus. Along with the cries, she heard a few, frightened children saying in scared high pitched tones: "I want my mom! I want my mom!"

The white pickup truck was in the median lane, slightly infringing in her lane, head on. Judging by the spray of debris from the back of the truck, the driver must have done a 360-degree spin in the middle of the icy road before stopping, facing oncoming traffic. The driver's side windshield was cracked like a spider-web. The front of the pickup truck was crumpled, all the way to the front tires, bare metal from the inside of the hood exposed, and the gray grill and dark engine in plain view. Steam was flowing out a split radiator hose, filling the air with white steam over the beat-up engine. Parts of the front of the truck littered the asphalt ground.

Addie pulled into the median of the road, just beyond the accident. She got out of her car, when she saw the driver of the pickup truck. He was standing outside of the open, driver's side door of the pickup. Addie asked in a loud and assertive voice, "Are you the driver of the pickup?"

"Yes," he quickly replied.

Addie scanned the inside of the truck, examining for interior damage and then quickly assessed the driver. The driver was a muscular, well-groomed man, with a close haircut, in his thirties. He wore a blue plaid flannel shirt, jeans, and rugged boots. He was pleasant and grateful to her. Addie noticed that he was not bleeding nor did he have any obvious injury. He seemed oriented and was able to talk to her. He was shaken from the accident. His voice was shaking and cutting off after each word. Addie could tell he was holding back from crying.

He said to Addie, "Yeah, I just hydroplaned and started spinning, I ran right into the bus, smashing it really hard. I already checked on them, and the woman on the bus said she was calling 911."

Addie carefully walked up to the yellow school bus. The road was full of debris that had been ejected from the back of the pickup truck. The debris, now sunken in a few inches of icy slush, had become obstacles in the road. It was obvious that the man used his pickup as a work truck, from the aerosol cans, metal joints, wire, tools, outlet covers, and other stuff possibly an electrician would use, scattered on the roadway. The road was growing increasingly icy and slippery by the moment. Addie's feet, in her black and white zebra-print clogs, kept sliding out to the side of her. "Oh, thank God, I didn't wear high heels! Me sprawled on the ground, that would be another ambulance en route."

Addie approached the bus. She noticed the bus driver walking around, examining the damage to the outside of the bus. His wiry grey hair and a bushy grey beard added to the pasty color of the man's wrinkled face. She concluded, after surveying the driver dripping in blood, that small pieces of glass were embedded in his face and arms. No real lacerations or gashes, but a lot of small cuts. The glass must have broken with such force from the impact of the, out of control, pickup truck. The tempered square glass fragments pierced his face and arms. Based on mechanism alone, and his age, he needed to be seen at the hospital. From the blood dripping down his arm, the sleeves of his red plaid flannel shirt must have been rolled up at the time of the accident. "Not relevant, just an observation," she thought. "He should be fine."

Addie stood at the open door of the bus, calling to a woman inside. "Hi. I'm a nurse, can I help?" Addie hastily observed the children inside the bus, to see if any required immediate medical attention. They all seem alert. The woman, who appeared to be in her sixties, was marked by excessive wrinkles and grey hair. Her obviously hard life had just become harder. She was trying to call 911, with difficulty. She kept pressing buttons and looking at the phone and trying again to place the call to 911. But she was too upset to even remember the name of the major road they were on. The woman glimpsed down at Addie's badge, and then gazing back up at Addie, asked, "Where are we? What's the address here?"

Addie turned to survey the house across the street for the house number. The first house she looked at did not have visible numbers; with the snow falling in her face she could not see. Then Addie scrutinized the neighboring house. "It's 1803, tell them 1800 Andrew Howard Parkway and we have a bus full of handicapped children and will need several ambulances." The frantic woman finally got the call to go through to 911.

The ice was coming down hard. Not only was it cold, it was sharp, and painful when it hit her face. Addie walking around the outside of the bus to make sure nothing was catching fire or dangerous at the scene of the accident. She did not notice any smell of diesel or fluids leaking from the engine that was bashed in on the driver's side. The worst damage was to the side of the bus, at the driver's seat and first two passenger bench seats. The yellow bus was completely crumpled on the side, yellow paint missing from the deep creases of the large dents. The lady on the bus said to Addie as she returned to the door, "I want to get the children out, somewhere safe."

Addie turned, looking at the sidewalk behind her, covered in inches of ice pellets, "Let's just keep the children on the bus until medics arrive or until we feel the bus is no longer safe." Addie stood on the steps inside the badly damaged bus, keeping some distance so as not to scare the mentally-challenged adolescents. She noticed the first two bench seats were crooked and twisted toward the aisle. She counted, thinking to herself, "Okay, I have four mentally handicapped adolescents/teens, one adult female caretaker in her sixties and one bus driver, around his sixties as well." She briskly inspected each one a second time. Not marking any bleeding or deformity in any of the children, she did notice one thing about all of them, even the caretaker woman. They all look scared, especially one young girl around age ten; she looked the most frightened. She held a serious expression with wide eyes and tight closed mouth with pursed lips on her childish rounded face. The young girl sat perfectly still in her seat. A young teenage boy, maybe around 12 years old, sat in the front seat. He seemed excited; his face pale, his eyes wide with surprise and his mouth gaping in awe. He seemed like he wanted to say something, but lacked the means to say what he was thinking. Jumping around in a seated position, he turned his head quickly and leaned his body in, to look at the driver's side broken window. He looked surprised to see the shattered glass covering the driver's seat. If he could have spoken, perhaps he would have asked her if she saw all the broken glass, too. The same boy then quickly turned to peek over his friend's seat at the spider-webbed side window. He peeped at the woman, almost for reassurance that they were all fine. By this time the older woman had the children calmed so they were no longer crying. None of the mentally disabled children said anything to Addie.

Not wanting to scare them, she kept her distance, but reassured them, "The police and ambulances are on the way, I will stay until they arrive." Addie had been told by her mother that she had a gift of calmly taking over situations, bringing assertiveness and control, making those who were upset to feel reassured with the knowledge that they are being helped. She did not want the driver or caretaker woman or the disabled children to feel that they were alone.

Addie exited the bus, but remained standing at the open bus doors. The driver had taken the top off of a road flare; his hands were shaking causing him to strike the flare a few times trying to get it to light. He kept his gaze focused on the flare, having tunnel vision, he was momentarily unaware Addie was standing in front of him. He finally struck the flare causing it to light. There was a loud flush sound, he jumped a little, from the flare igniting, emitting a tall orange glow of flame. With his shaking hands, he placed two flares at the front of the bus so oncoming traffic would see them. The icy snow was heavily hitting Addie and the bus driver while they stood in the road, both patiently waiting for police and ambulances to arrive. Addie realized she was no longer cold and she was no longer hungry.

She was concerned for the people involved in the accident, they all seemed so distraught. Shaking and trying to do simple tasks such as calling 911 and lighting flares posed a challenge. Hoping she was right about the mechanism of injury, and pretty sure no one was suffering life threatening injuries, her experience as a trauma nurse told her that the icy roadway had prevented both vehicles from traveling at a high rate of speed. She sensed that the vehicles had taken the impact and not the passengers inside. But she hated to see the fear the mentally challenged children were exhibiting.

Barely visible in the snow, a man wearing a navy blue sweatshirt and navy pants trudged towards her. She could see a black SUV with flashing lights down the road beyond the crash, but could not make out what kind of vehicle it was. As he got closer, she could see a radio attached to his shoulder and she was able to read his sweatshirt, Police K-9. "I'm K-9 from the city. County police are on the way but I heard the call come out and was right down the road. Is everyone okay?"

Addie replied: "Yes, officer, there are four mentally challenged adolescents, one female care provider in her sixties, and the bus driver, in his sixties. Significant damage to the inside of the bus. There is one driver in the pickup truck, and some damage inside his vehicle as well. We will need several ambulances for transport."

The officer got on his radio. He was too soft spoken for Addie to hear what he was telling the police dispatcher. Ambulance sirens with yelps and wails were coming around the corner and up the median, fighting the congested four lane road. On-coming traffic was making U-turns because of the debris closing their two lanes, creating further chaos of an already dangerous situation. As soon as the first ambulance arrived, Addie asked the K-9 officer, "Are you okay then? I'm going to leave since the medics have arrived."

The officer, still on his radio answered, "Yeah, I'm good. I'm leaving as soon as county police arrive. Thanks."

Addie climbed back in her car and drove off. As she drove, realizing she was now an hour late meeting Frank at the hospital, she hoped he was safe. Calling his phone again, reaching his voicemail, she rolled her eyes at the sound of his voice - his clear, deep masculine voice. "You have reached Detective Knight, please leave a message." She left a quick message: "Hey, it's Addie, I'm running late but I'm on my way. Bye."

Her hunger returned in a fury, making up for the lost time at the bus accident. All of her muscles felt tense; she felt the cold penetrating through her saturated clothes. Her full-bodied blond hair was plastered to her head. While driving, she quickly glanced in the rear-view mirror, "Ugh, blondes never look good wet."

Stuck in more traffic, driving between ten and twenty miles per hour in the icy, slushy streets, she returned to watching the snow, falling like stars from the sky. She turned on the radio; "Bitter Sweet Symphony" by The Verve was playing. *I let the melody shine, let it cleanse my mind, I feel free now.* It was strange how certain songs seemed to play on the radio at just the right moment. She supposed that it was what the psychologist Carl Jung would have described as synchronicity.

Addie pondered to herself. "Why was I the only one to pull over? All of those people driving by...no one stopped, no one offered to call 911, or see if the children were okay. It's nurses, police, firemen, and medics; we are the only ones that run towards danger when everyone else is either ignoring it or running away. There is not much difference between someone who was sexually assaulted and someone who has been in a severe car accident, fire, or mass casualty shooting. Each day begins as if it is any other day, with ourselves and everyone we love, thinking we will make it home safely. Even that minor accident, without life threatening injuries, temporarily created chaos and fear."

She inched along on the snow-covered streets, thinking to herself: "It is fear that causes you to lose trust; be it a loss of trust in yourself, in family, or in faith. Not only do you lose trust in the friend or family member who victimized you, but you might lose trust in your home, work, or school, in which you were assaulted. More importantly, not only do you lose trust, but you lose your gauge for when to feel fear. You are not sure when to be afraid, so every situation creates fear. Checking the locks on the doors and windows to make sure they are locked, and then going back to check them all over again becomes the norm of someone who has lost trust in themselves. Our loved ones may view this behavior as paranoid, but it's not paranoia at all, it is fear. Fear causing you to no longer think clearly and freely, leaving the mind void of rational thought. The home or work environment, what they once knew as safe, is no longer a predictable, safe place to live. Keeping the volume on the TV or radio to a minimum, afraid to not miss an alerting sound. Afraid of an intruder breaking into their home again, coming back to 'finish the job.' Afraid of a gunman in the hallway of school or work, killing classmates or co-worker's, again. Suddenly a trigger is released, maybe a sudden, unexpected loud sound. You startle and jump, a flushing sensation overcomes you, your pulse is pounding, you are in an instant frenzy, unable to think rationally, and then you realize the loud noise was just a truck driving past. Life is a bittersweet symphony, isn't it?"

Brake lights shining on the snowy, slushy road, snapped Addie back to reality, "Alright, enough with such heavy thoughts. I wish the snow would stop. I am so late, and my phone is almost dead. Frank is probably wondering where the hell I am. Traffic sucks.

Nothing to do now, except drive slowly and be patient. Damn, I'm hungry, and no place to stop. Shit, I am exhausted, too. Nice language from a Catholic girl. I need a nap."

With the snow coming down and visibility poor, traffic was even slower. Trying to stay awake, and not focusing on how hungry she was, she drove and enjoyed her time of free thought and singing to the radio.

The bluetooth ringing through the speakers jolted Addie out of her reverie, as she answered her phone through the steering wheel. "Hello, this is Addie."

She heard Sergeant Moran's voice. "Hey girl, it's Kate. I haven't talked to you in a while, and just wanted to catch up. We've had some pretty bad cases lately. But we arrested the guys that assaulted Todd Meadows."

"Oh, thank God! They were not going to stop until they were caught. Kate, I was just thinking how nurses, detectives, and prosecuting attorneys, who have chosen to work with victims of crimes, have chosen a career that requires compassion and empathy. Those who lack compassion and empathy usually don't enjoy this line of work. It's truly a gift, isn't it?"

Sergeant Kate replied, "Yes, it is. I have always felt patrol officers are the first line of defense for victims of crime. If we, the police, can't prevent crime then at least we have to find and arrest the bad guys."

"We can never deny anyone the right to have their trust renewed and to feel safe again," Addie responded. "Our patients, the victims, reach out for a hand to hold onto."

"We can hope that victims of these horrible assaults can gain trust in humanity again," sighed Kate.

"I guess that's why they say 'trust is where peace flows.' And there's nothing like good police work! Congratulations on your arrest. Hey, how about you come over tonight and hang out with Rachel and me?"

"Thanks, I'll try and stop by some time this evening." And Kate bade her goodbye as her phone clicked off.

Driving up the hill to the hospital, snow blanketed the ground while decorating the tops of the tree branches. "Oh, how serene," she mused to herself. The road was coated in a thin layer of ice and snow. "Finally, I'm here, and an hour and a half late. But, I do love the snow and I really don't mind being out in it either."

As Addie approached the door she saw it swing open as Jerry the security guard held it for her.

"Thanks, Jerry! You're certainly dedicated to be here on such an icy day. I bet they did not have days like this where you're from."

"No, ma'am," replied Jerry, his piercing blue-gray eyes scrutinizing her, questioningly. "I guess you're here to meet with Detective Knight. He's been waiting for about an hour or so. I hope you did not have any trouble on the road."

"Oh, I did, but everything's alright. Thanks, Jerry." Addie strode down the long corridor to the forensic department. Only police and forensic nurses had access to the secured department. Frank was pacing in the lobby at the main entrance. Looking at his phone then down the adjacent hallways, he seemed quite concerned about Addie's unusual lateness. Then he beheld Addie walking down the hall towards him. Trying not to appear too anxious, he failed miserably.

Addie's coat was wet; her hair, damp and straight. Her cheeks were still scarlet from the icy cold air hitting her face at the bus accident. He touched her arm, regarding her with a slight crease of worry in his brow. "Where were you? The roads are really icy. I was afraid you ran off the road or something."

"Yeah, something like that. Traffic was a big delay but a school bus, with mentally challenged children, was involved in an accident. I stopped to make sure they were okay and I waited for EMS to arrive. I'm really sorry I'm late, but my phone was almost dead. Did you get my message? I forgot to charge my phone this morning. It's been quite a day!"

"I heard the call go out over the police scanner for that accident, I think four medics responded. It sounded pretty bad. I'm glad you stopped to help, I would have, too. I saw that you called but I didn't know you left a message."

He suddenly leaned over to give her a quick hug. She smiled, and nodded her head in the direction of her office. "Let's go to my office and look over this chart. I think when we're finished here, I'm going back home. I'm going to take a hot bath put my pajamas back on and watch TV with Rachel for the rest of the snowy day. I hear we're really going to get hit with more snow tonight. I really should watch the news more."

As soon as they entered the secured, private hallway to Addie's office, Frank exclaimed with joy, "We made an arrest! We got 'em, both of them!" Gazing directly into Addie's eyes, placing his hands on her shoulders, and smiling, Frank exclaimed, "Me and the other detectives and Sergeant Moran, well, Kate, we all worked thirty hours straight, looking at every bit evidence. The woman who found Todd at the park and ride, she was able to give a partial tag and so we found them. We also found video surveillance of them. The gun and stun gun were still in the car. Blue cord was found in the console. We found Todd's license in the front console; the dumbasses had the license right between the two of them. And yeah Addie, they did stink, and the one with crazy gold teeth, damn, he's ugly. They will be tried in two separate trials, but we got 'em."

Addie beamed with triumph. "Looks like celebratory drinks are in order! I wish we could go out tonight, but the snow is coming." She gave Frank a sideways glance and a wink. "But you can call me tonight. We'll have drinks over the phone."

His brow furrowed, as if it was not what he had in mind. She chuckled. Without a word, Addie walked over to a big leather chair, and sat behind the tidy desk. Frank pulled up a chair next to her. Reading page by page of her seventeen page forensic report, they remain focused on the brutal assault.

"Let's start with the body map of his injuries. He had bruising to the top of his head; it was difficult to see at first glance because his hair concealed the contusions. The contusion or bruise measured 1.5 cm by 4 cm, possibly from the butt of the gun. The laceration to his forehead was five centimeters in length, which needed eight sutures to close. He has a nasal fracture. I found several sets of burn patterns consistent with a two prong stun gun, making direct contact with his back at least four times.

"I photographed all of the injuries to his face, the burns, the anal tears and the ligature marks to both his wrists. I already uploaded them and I didn't see anything new. So the body map is accurate. The ligature was wrapped around both of his wrists three times, and uptake of toluidine was positive for acute injury. I also had uptake of toluidine around his anus, and the burns to his back, also confirming acute injury. I think we have it all. Just have to wait to see if they take the plea deal, if it's even offered, or wait for the trial date."

Frank asked Addie, "So, the laceration to his forehead, what can you tell me about that? Was it from the gun or fists?"

"Just by looking at the laceration, before it was sutured, I can only tell you that it's from blunt force trauma. The force from being hit by a fist or the butt of the gun will give the same result, tearing of the skin and tissue layer with an irregular border. His injury had tissue bridging, which is seen only in blunt force trauma. Mr. Meadows' skin surface was hit with such force that it split apart leaving some areas with fine skin threads still attached, which is the bridging.

"Mr. Meadows is not a large man, but even so, the stun gun will take any man out, no matter the size. The immediate overload of lactic acid in the muscles from being shocked renders anyone temporarily incapacitated and confused. Those guys were serious about causing some grievous bodily harm. I'm glad you and your team of detectives caught them."

"Addie, thanks for your report. Let's get out of here and get you home."

Addie pulled off her now dry coat from the coat rack in her office. She handed Frank his coat as well. Turning off the lights and locking the unit, she hoped no sexual assaults would occur on that cold snowy day. "I'm parked in the garage, just outside the hospital entrance, so I can walk through the hospital and right to my car. We're not supposed to park there, but not many visitors today."

"I'll walk you to your car." Frank chatted away in excitement about the case, telling Addie again how they caught the suspects who so brutally attacked Todd Meadows and other gay men in the Baltimore/Washington, DC area.

As they approached Addie's car, she felt she did not want to leave him. "How annoyed I am with how the weather has ruined a date night with him," she thought. "We always are so at ease together. All the previous times we went out with work friends, but there were too many people around. I don't want to leave. I have no desire driving in the complete opposite direction from him." She viewed Frank, smiling, studying the features of his face, his eyes. He had some darkness under his eyes; she realized he was also tired from the long, stressful weekend. She knew he needed to catch up on much needed sleep. He stopped talking and looked into her eyes, then he bent forward to kiss her. She felt like she would melt; she felt a rush in her head. Frank had become the first thing she thought about when she woke up and the last thing she thought about when she went to sleep. Shaking her head, she politely backed away. "We need to stop but just for now. Call me later."

"No, you call me as soon as you get home, so I know you got

home safely." Frank gently kissed her on the forehead. She closed her eyes and hugged Frank, taking a deep breath in order to absorb every bit of him. He had a clean, fresh smell.

"I'm going home from here," he said. "Maybe have a few beers and catch up on TV. Spring weather in Baltimore…it will be hot and humid before you know it."

One year after the assault of Todd Meadows the suspects were tried separately. The victim, detectives, and Addie were subpoenaed to testify in the two trials. Each trial was one week long. Both suspects were found guilty by two separate juries and each were sentenced to serve 50 years in prison.

Chapter Five: Forever in a Chimney

"Life is pleasant. Death is peaceful. It's the transition that's troublesome." —Isaac Asimov

Eddie Dalton was hanging out with his high school friends, Lucas and Tom, talking about their summer jobs and plans for college in the fall. The flat roof on the back of an old church was their favorite hangout. No one could see them from the main road because of the woods in the back. Tonight, the sky was clear with an abundance of stars in the sky.

"Hey," Tom said. "Look over here, there's a chimney and it opens into the church. I bet we could get into the church through the chimney. Eddie, you're the thinnest, how 'bout you climb down and open the door to let us in?"

"Hell, no!" replied Eddie. "What if I get stuck? That's a stupid idea. Let's just hang out here, on the roof."

Lucas spoke, hesitantly. "I don't know, I think it would be kinda cool to have an abandoned church all to ourselves. Once we get in and pry a door open or break a window for access, it's all ours. Eddie, come on, nothin' to it, just shimmy down the chimney and you're in."

"No!" exclaimed Eddie. "What if bats or something is living in there. I don't want to do it! I hate small spaces."

"Man, last summer, I helped clean chimneys as my summer job," mused Tom. "It's not that bad. I would go in them all the time. They narrow toward the bottom, but your skinny ass should have no problem getting through. Just do it! Stop acting like a little girl."

Lucas, making fun of Eddie, chanted, "Oh, stopppp itttt, I don't want to get my clothes dirty."

Eddie reluctantly agreed. "Here is my wallet and I don't want to break my cell phone. I'll leave them here. But if you hear me screaming, you better get help, got it?"

Tom and Lucas, simultaneously chimed, "Yeah, yeah, you got it. We'll help you."

Eddie climbed into the top of the chimney, despondent at his friends' insistence, still feeling it was a terrible idea. The opening was huge. "Huh, maybe this ain't so bad after all. I will slowly climb down. Oh cool, there's even a ladder. Piece of cake. I don't know what I was so worried about. I got this."

The chimney's metal rungs sticking out from the mortar stopped. Eddie called, "Hey guys, the ladder stopped, I'm going to jump down the rest of the way."

Tom shouted, "No! Don't, Eddie! If the ladder stops it means the chimney is too narrow. Don't! Climb back up." Tom's heart was racing; he was in a panic as he suddenly remembered the downside of chimney cleaning: it was a dangerous and unpredictable job.

Eddie, unconscious from the hitting his head as he fell, was unable to call or speak. His friends assumed he made it through and was in the church. Tom and Lucas walked the perimeter of the church, looking in the windows for any sign of Eddie. Meanwhile, in the front of the abandoned church, a police car drove by and stopped. As the boys saw the white lights of the patrol car backing up, they froze. The police officer got out, and called to them. "Hey, come over here! What are your names?"

"Uh, I'm Tom,"

"And I'm Lucas."

"What are you two doing?" asked the police officer.

Tom scratched his head. "Nothing officer, we are on our way home and wanted to check out the church. It looked pretty cool, kinda creepy with the tall grass and overgrown weeds. We're just messing around."

The police officer folded his arms. "You're on your way home?"

Lucas nodded. "Yes, sir."

Police officer said, sternly, "Get on outta here before I cite you for trespassing."

Several weeks later, the church grounds crew prepared the church for summer bible camp, mowing the lawn and removing the overgrown vines.

"Man, what's that smell?" gasped one worker.

Turning off the lawn mower to reply, another man said, "I don't know, maybe an animal died in the back. It's hot as hell out, what a miserable week. It's been over 100 degrees every day. Let's just finish, I want to get to a cold beer and my pool."

"Yeah, we don't get paid enough to remove dead animals. A cold beer sounds good right about now."

One hot day in early summer, it was Rachel's last shift as a death investigator. The intense heat had made her decision to change jobs much easier and very welcomed. It was 5 o'clock in the afternoon, still 90 degrees, and Rachel sat in the air-conditioned apartment in Fell's Point, protected from the heat and humidity. She and Addie had rented a movie and planned on ordering take-out for dinner, since it was too hot to do anything outside.

"I love this movie and you'll love it, too," Addie was saying as she slid the disc into the DVD player. "I can't believe you've never seen it!"

"It's a movie filmed in Baltimore, right? What's it called again?" asked Rachel.

"*Ladder 49*," responded Addie, making herself cozy on the sofa with a glass of chilled white wine. "John Travolta and Joaquin Phoenix are in it. It's about firefighters in Baltimore. The main part of the movie is when Joaquin Phoenix's character gets trapped in a large warehouse fire in Baltimore City. It will keep you on the edge of your seat, you'll love it!"

Rachel speculated that the film would probably make her think of David, the firefighter whom she had once fallen in love with but who had disappeared after their first date. "I'll probably cry," she said aloud. But she poured herself some iced tea and became engrossed in the movie.

Rachel's phone rang, breaking her concentration. She recognized the number of the police dispatcher as she answered. The officer on the other end of the phone stated, "Hi Rachel, we need you to respond to a church on the east side of the county. A body has been found in an old chimney that was sealed up many years ago."

Rachel turned to Addie, "I have to go to a death scene. Apparently, a body is trapped in a chimney."

"What?" exclaimed Addie, turning off the movie. "That sounds horrendous. You may need the help of the fire department. I wonder if anyone has called them."

"Good idea. Let me get over there and see what's going on." As Rachel pulled her navy-blue T-shirt with the Forensic Investigator patch over her blond curls she realized that it was probably the last time she would wear the shirt. She had really found the past nine years working the job to be a privilege. She had learned a lot about a topic that few people know about, or even want to know about. She wound up in places she never thought she would be in and made some long-lasting friendships.

Pulling up at the church, Rachel observed more than the usual number of police cars and fire apparatus that respond to a death scene. So someone had already called the fire department. Gazing at the church, she marveled at the old magnificent brick building. Attached to the rear of the church was a single-story brick building with a flat roof that seemed to have been added at a later date.

Ignoring the television cameras, she strode into the church asking, "Who's the primary officer?" Everyone pointed to Detective Andrews, a new detective who had only been working in homicide for one week.

Rachel walked up to Detective Andrews, smiling, "Hi, I'm Rachel. I hear you transferred from the sex crimes unit. I guess you know Sergeant Kate Moran? Boy, this is some case to have as your first!"

The ghost of a smile flickered on Detective Andrew's face as he earnestly shook her hand. He gave Rachel the CC number and informed her of the background of the case. "The church was preparing for a two-week long summer bible camp for neighborhood children. One of the grounds workers noticed some bugs on the floor in the hallway. The church called in an exterminator who traced the bugs back to a locked room. When he asked what is in the room and how he could access it, a lady in the office, Mrs. Lynch, located the keys."

"Hmm" mused Rachel. "What is the room used for, why is it locked?"

"It has an old chimney that hasn't been used in probably twenty years," the young detective replied. "A grate covers the bottom of it so that nobody can access the opening, but the room is kept locked to prevent anyone from trying. When the exterminator approached the room he said he noticed a foul smell. Upon entering the room, the exterminator saw legs and feet through the grate. He ran to the office and called 911."

Rachel nodded. "Let's have a look."

"I'll lead the way," said Detective Andrews.

Upon entering the small, swelteringly hot room Rachel noticed a metal grate, approximately 18 inches high and 18 inches wide, on the bottom of the wall directly across from the door. There were maggots crawling around on the ground. Moving in for a closer look, Rachel identified the bottom of two legs and two feet through the grate. A pair of blue jeans was visible, bunched around the ankles.

Rachel backed out of the stifling room and turned to Detective Andrews. "Let me take a few pictures and we can talk with the commanding officer from the fire department to see about getting us access to the body."

Detective Andrews gave a slight bow of acquiescence. Rachel took her photos, noticing that the legs, pants and the entire inside of the grate were covered with maggots. She finished and faced Detective Andrews, asking, "Any ideas on how to get him out of there?"

Without waiting for an answer, Rachel pivoted and left the small hot room, looking for the fire department personnel. Crime Lab and Homicide were trailing in her wake, all eager to figure out the plan and wait in the cool air conditioning of their car.

Rachel approached the commanding officer of the fire department, Lieutenant Willis. "Any suggestions on how to get this body out of the wall, Lieutenant?"

Lieutenant Willis curtly replied, "I think the best idea would be to call for the fire department's confined space team, the CST." He abruptly stopped talking, keyed his radio and asked for the team to be dispatched to the location. Everyone scattered to sit in their cars and wait.

Recalling that David had told her that he was on the confined space team, Rachel's heart jumped as she walked over to her car. She wondered if David would be there. She had heard through the grapevine that he was back in town from wherever he had been. Perspiration already trickled down her back, glistening on her arms and face, causing her blond curls to be plastered against her head.

What a shame if David came and here she was, such a mucky mess! But she pushed the frustration from her mind as she sat in her cool car, sipping some iced tea from her thermos. She was a medical professional with a job to do. It did not matter, under the circumstances, if she was not at her most attractive. She was there to identify a corpse so that a fellow human being could have a decent burial.

Thirty minutes passed before two additional fire trucks pulled up in front of the church. David jumped out from the truck, his eyes quickly scanning the crowd. Rachel had told him that she was a death investigator. Was he searching for her? She inwardly kicked herself. The team of six firemen walked into the building to assess the situation. Knowing that the body was her responsibility, Rachel joined them with a determined air.

"Rachel!" David was smiling warmly at her, and held the door as she walked into the church. "I – I was wondering if you would be here."

Rachel waved her hand nonchalantly. "Nice to see you," she said, leaving him staring at her backside as she authoritatively marched into the building.

In a moment they were all gathered together near the reeking chimney. After discussing the situation with Lieutenant Willis, Detective Andrews and Rachel, the confined space team climbed up onto the roof of the building to assess the situation from above, to estimate the position of the body within the chimney. It was important for them to identify the location of the body in order to prevent mutilation of the body while opening the wall. The fire department commanded everyone to leave the immediate vicinity as they began to breach the wall, using sledge hammers and air operated demo hammers.

While waiting, Rachel called the transport team, the team that would take the body to the medical examiner's office. Listening to all of the noise and commotion, she wished she could sneak back in and watch the fire department work. In about forty minutes the noise stopped, and David came out; taking off his helmet, his face glistened with perspiration. He announced: "We've removed the bricks from the lower portion of the old chimney. The wall is open now, so you can get to the body." David regarded Rachel with a pensive expression as he removed his heavy turn-out coat. His shirt underneath was soaking wet.

Rachel was aware that they had to wear their coats for protection. But she leaned towards David, whispering, "I don't know how you can do the work you do, in such a small, closed-in space that's so hot while wearing so much clothing."

David shrugged his muscular shoulders. "You get used to it."

Rachel put on a Tyvek jacket given to her by Crime Lab since there were so many maggots. Followed by a group of homicide detectives, she pulled on her gloves and re-entered the small, airless room. Through the opening in the wall Rachel saw a body standing with its feet on the floor, its arms dangling down by its sides and its upper body leaning forward with shoulders and forehead against the wall in front of it. A pair of blue jeans were wrapped around the feet and ankles; a pair of blue boxer shorts were on the pelvic area. It's possible, Rachel thought, that he dropped his jeans to cool off as he began to overheat.

After taking many photographs, Rachel spread a sheet over the floor in front of the opening and prepared to pull the body out. As she grabbed the boxer shorts, she realized that the entire pelvic area was alive with movement; it was a mass of writhing maggots. Rachel supported the shoulders as she pulled the body up and out towards her, intending to place it on the sheet. Suddenly, Rachel felt resistance and was unable to move the body any further.

"Damn," she mumbled under her breath. "It's stuck." Rachel turned towards the detectives who had been gathered in a group behind her, waiting to examine the body once it was on the sheet. "Can someone please give me a hand?"

All of the sudden, Rachel realized she was the only one left in the room; everyone else had vanished into the hallway. She poked her head around the corner and repeated, "Can someone please help me pull this body out?" Nobody offered assistance. David had disappeared.

Rachel thought she would just have to wait until the transport team arrived; they would help her. Suddenly, someone pushed through the small crowd. David volunteered his assistance. "Sorry, I was called away. But I'm back now."

Rachel smiled her gratitude, "Thanks. His feet are stuck. If you could just grab his feet I think he will come out easily." Rachel and David pulled the body out of the opening and onto the sheet that is laid out on the floor. All of the sudden, the crowd hurried back into the room to examine the body with her. First, Rachel shot additional photographs of the body. She documented her observations on her clipboard: very thin male body with no shoes, no shirt, blue jeans bunched around his ankles and blue boxer shorts that still remained on his pelvic area. The skin on his face appeared dry, ashy-black in color and leathery. Rigor has passed, but she was unable to determine lividity. The skin on his body was also grayish-black in color with large masses of maggots noted on the entire body, especially in the pelvic area. She rolled the body over, photographing all sides, knowing that it would be difficult to identify any small injuries due to the advanced stage of decomposition.

The transport team had arrived. Rachel greeted them. "Thanks for responding quickly. He's all yours. I didn't find any identification on him so he will go in as an unknown male. Maybe they can find his identity by searching the missing persons database, or they can put a sketch artist's drawing of him on the news. Hopefully someone will recognize him. He's been here for a while; somebody must be looking for him." Handing a piece of paper to them, she continued, "Here, I wrote the case number down for you."

Once the body was loaded into the transport van and on the way to the medical examiner's office, Rachel thanked the fire department, police department and crime lab personnel who remained at the scene. With mixed emotions she headed to the welcoming coolness of her car. She heard footsteps behind her and pirouetted to face David.

"Rachel. Let's catch up. Could we meet for a drink sometime soon? "

Rachel yawned, covering her mouth. "Excuse me." She opened the door of her car. "Sorry, I am really busy with the new forensic nursing program. I'm not sure what my schedule is anymore." David held the door as she climbed in and started the engine. His face was fallen, as if stabbed to the heart. She gave him an encouraging smile. "Well, I still have your number in my phone. I'll give you a call next week. It would be good to see you again."

"Thanks, Rachel." David sounded truly grateful. "Maybe by then we'll know who that poor guy in the chimney is."

Rachel nodded, slammed the door, and drove away with the air conditioner going full blast. All she could think of at that moment was the shower. In a few minutes, she was on the highway, heading towards Fell's Point. She found herself pondering David. She had forgotten how deep his eyes were; she kept picturing his eyes and his face as she drove home.

The following morning, Addie was in the kitchen making apple pancakes and bacon. As the two friends enjoyed breakfast Addie enquired, "How'd it go last night? Someone died in a chimney?"

Finishing her bite of pancake and wiping her mouth, Rachel replied, "Yeah, we don't know who he is or why he was in the chimney. It really was a very sad case."

"Of course it was your last case as a death investigator. Will you ever know what happened to him?" Addie asked.

Putting the dishes in the sink, Rachel said, "I will never know why he was stuck in the chimney."

Addie poured another cup of coffee. "I'm on call today. I hope it's quiet."

"I plan to do nothing today. Oh, and the best part, I saw David last night! We chatted a bit." Winking to Addie, Rachel could feel her heartrate speed up.

Chapter 6: Who Has Time for a Bomb Threat?

"Every man is guilty of all the good he did not do." —*Voltaire*

Addie was in the office finishing the case of a two-year-old child who was sexually assaulted earlier in the day. The forensics office was conveniently located outside of the emergency room. The ER was in controlled chaos and, as always, extremely busy. The conditions inside of the emergency room were loud with indistinct talking of police, doctors, and nurses. Some patients' family members were standing in the doorways, wondering why it was taking so long for their family member to be seen, occasionally calling out to inquire how much longer the wait would be. The phone rang off the hook.

Police and medics arrived with a young woman, Beth Walter, who claimed to have been raped while at a party. After being placed in room 8, behind the closed door, Detective Knight began interviewing Beth. Charles, Beth's boyfriend, waited in the hallway outside of the room.

Addie wandered back to the ER to see if any other sexual assaults had arrived. She glanced up, surprised to see Charles, Cain's brother, standing in the hallway. Happy to see an old friend, she called, "Hi, Charles, my God, I haven't seen you in ages! How's Cain? I guess he's graduated from law school? And finally landed a job?"

Charles came over and gave her a friendly hug. He was almost as handsome as Cain, but much younger. "Cain's good. He works for the law firm of MacIntyre and Ross, which is not too far from here."

"Well, that's great, I'm happy for him, that he's doing well and all. I haven't talked to him since, I don't know, since shortly after he broke off our wedding."

Charles looked confused. "He said that *you* broke up with *him*?"

Addie shook her head. "No. He told me that he couldn't marry me and he wanted the ring back. It's a long story. We had our time together but then our time was up. Our personalities were great together. He was the best thing that ever happened to me, but a few years into our relationship, our careers seemed to get in the way. Please, tell Cain that I said 'hi' and I would love to see him for coffee since we work so close to each other. Can you give him my number?" Pulling off a paper towel, she wrote down her phone number, handing it to Charles.

Addie then noticed that her longtime friend Vicki, the ER secretary, appeared to be extremely flustered. Addie and Vicki had worked together at Trauma One Regional Center. Through stress and tragedy, they formed a bonding friendship. On rare nights, while working at the trauma center, they would sneak up to the helipad, enjoying a cup of coffee and cigarette. Occasionally, a few of the young resident doctors on their trauma rotation would join the girls. The trauma helipad was a unique view of the city. Amid the violence destroying human dignity, Baltimore shimmered with city lights, luminous and magnificent under the black depths of the night sky.

"Vicki, what's wrong?" Addie could read her feelings of being overwhelmed by the tears in her eyes and her frantic movements, unsure which way to go next.

Vicki, visibly shaking, came over to Addie. "Addie, we have to move everyone out, there's been a bomb threat called into the ER. Get your patient; I think she's in room 8. I want both of you to get out of here."

Frank ducked in. "What's going on?"

"It's a bomb threat. Vicki took the call," Addie informed him.

Frank calmly turned to Vicki. "Tell me exactly what he said."

Vicki, upset and absolutely ticked off, replied, "I answered the phone the way I always do. But my dentures had come loose; I don't think I used enough denture cream before coming to work, and the constant answering of the damn phones, the top fell on the lower, making a bit of a clatter. A man on the other line replied, in a sweetly quiet voice, so quiet I had to turn up the volume on my phone. He said: 'Listen carefully. I placed a bomb in the emergency room. I love the look of fear on your face right now. Now, now, don't look around. You can't see me. But I. Can. See. *You!*' Suddenly, the caller burst into a really intrusive, loud voice. 'Don't find out the hard way. Don't use the phone. You don't wanna blow up, do you? What did you say your name was...Vicki?' Then he yelled in a deep guttural growl. 'Well, Vicki, there is a bomb in the emergency room!' Chills ran down my spine. I tried to listen for any identification from his voice. I tried to keep the caller on the phone for as long as I could but I drew a blank in asking him questions. But I listened to the sound of his voice and noises in his background. I tried to follow the script, which I was taught by Cheryl, the night shift nurse manager of the emergency room, for if a bomb threat is ever called in. I wish Cheryl was on duty tonight and had answered that phone. She can easily sense bullshit. She would have ripped that guy a new asshole. We are too busy for this crap! And now we have to clear all these patients outta here? After the caller hung up, I screamed out for Madison. I was too afraid to use the phone to overhead page."

"Madison's in charge tonight?" Addie inquired.

"Yeah." Vicki, turning to Frank, explained that the charge nurse is sometimes different each night. "Madison, when running charge of the emergency room, can control chaos. All of the charge nurses are used to controlling life-threatening circumstances. No doubt she's already called 911."

Madison's voice rang over the intercom system. "I need all nurses and doctors to report to the nurses station STAT! I repeat, I need all nurses and doctors to report to the nurses station STAT!" Frank hurried back to the victim in room 8. Addie and Vicki joined the others. Addie noticed Jerry, the security guard, standing behind Madison. She had not seen him all morning and thought that he was not on duty. Jerry had shown himself to be helpful on several levels, from making coffee runs to being willing to sit outside the room of female rape patients. He would offer kind words to victims and often sit with girls while they waited for the forensic nurse and police to arrive at the hospital.

In a huddle of nurses and doctors, charge nurse Madison notified the staff. "A bomb threat has been called in. Vicki took the call and the police have already been notified. All we know right now is that it was a male caller who stated that he placed a bomb in the ER. We suspect he was a patient earlier today, upset over the long wait, but we're not sure. We don't have any other information right now. We haven't seen any suspicious items but we need to take the call seriously. We need to evacuate the ER and get these patients out of here, now! Docs, if you can write up the patients who are ready for discharge, then we can send them home. Everyone else, we need to do a lateral move and move these patients down toward the operating rooms."

Addie noticed Dr. Emory, in his scrubs, standing on the periphery of the crowd with an odd, cynical grin, arms folded. Before she could process the oddness of his stance, he spun around and strode through the automatic sliding doors, heading towards the OR. Addie stood in front of Vicki, offering a reassuring smile. "Don't worry, Vic, we'll all make it home safely, I'm sure. We'll be okay; hopefully, it's just a threat, but I want you to get yourself out of here and get down to the operating room with the others." Then she whispered, "Vicki, to make this night worse, Cain's brother, Charles, is here. It's his girlfriend who was sexually assaulted! I don't have a safe place that I can move her to. Detective Knight, who you just met, is working the case."

Vicki replied in a low voice. "Is he the detective you were telling me about last week?

Addie smiled and nodded.

"Addie, he is so nice looking. You go, girl!" smiling and nodding back, "I want details when things heat up. Now get your patient and get out of here."

Addie squeezed her hand. "Don't worry. You will get all the details."

Detective Knight emerged from room 8 after interviewing Beth. At the same moment, Madison walked up to Addie. "Addie, I'm so glad you're here. We're evacuating the ER for the bomb threat. I'm working on finding space near the operating rooms for your patient, but it's pretty full over there. I can't move you just yet. Jerry, with security, offered to stay with your patient. But I told him 'no', because you have a police officer. Then I told him that he needs to go to the OR with everyone else. I thought it was nice of him to offer."

Frank said to Madison, "As soon as you can, get them out of here!" Then he turned to Addie. "Do whatever you need to do to keep safe. The patrol officer is staying with you; he will maintain chain of custody, making sure evidence remains secure on Ms. Walters' clothing and body, especially since this emergency room is in total chaos." He stared at her with concern, knowing that if a bomb really was placed in the ER, Addie could be injured or killed.

Addie spoke after a split second of reflection. "Madison, I guess I have to stay behind in the ER until we find a safe place to move her? I can take photographs and get the details of the assault later, when we get to a safe area. I can be moved anywhere in the hospital, I just need quick medical clearance from the ER doc first. I'll start by collecting her blood and urine. Since I have a patrol officer to watch over her while I send off the labs and order meds, I don't need any other help. Just let me know where I can move her to. Thanks."

Madison nodded. "Thanks, Addie. I'm sorry you'll be the last to move out. I can't get your patient cleared because the ER doc is down in the OR holding area. Plus, Dr. Emory said that the holding area was full. He won't let you bring your patient down. You can't just take her to another area of the hospital; it's against protocol. The other patients need to go on monitors and I need the space in the OR with oxygen access and cardiac monitors for them. I have the hospital supervisor looking for a place to put you. There is so much bureaucracy, that I can't just put you in an empty room on another unit. It's horrible, I know."

Addie calmly replied, "So Dr. Emory would prefer that my patient and I die in an explosion rather than moving us out to a secured location?"

Madison rolled her eyes. "For now, I have only been given clearance to move priority two and priority three ER patients that are being admitted or need a further work-up, including cardiac monitoring and oxygen treatment, to the operating room recovery. Your patient doesn't fit into either protocol criteria, so the hospital supervisor wants you to stay put until we figure something out. Or until Dr. Emory makes space for you."

Frank said to Addie, "Get as much collected before you move her, but I know you'll do what's best. I have to get over to the crime scene with Sergeant Moran and make sure the crime lab collects the bedding and collects the contents from the bathroom trash can. Addie, just be careful but I want you to get out as soon as you can."

The emergency department hallways were congested with patients on stretchers and in wheelchairs with all staff moving briskly, trying to evacuate everyone as quickly as possible. The portable cardiac monitors on each stretcher were audibly announcing the heart beats of the patients. The heart beats were captured from wires clamped onto the round electrodes stuck to the patients' chests. The beeping of the monitors, not in succession with each other, were enough to drive one crazy. Police officers were everywhere, with the squelching of radio communication further adding to the noise in the emergency room. Police canvassed for any evidence of the bomb by going room by room, opening cabinets, looking under stretchers and in supply carts.

The police had called for a bomb sniffing dog. There entered a black and tan German shepherd wearing a black police K-9 vest that read "bomb squad" on one side and "Violet" on the other. Violet was one of the newest bomb-sniffing K-9's and had been called in to help in the search. Over the police radio many codes and squelches were heard, and then the clear radio of K-9 Officer Loren announcing: "K-9 beginning to clear rooms 1 and 2."

Addie did not want Charles to stay in the emergency department, but neither did she want to admit she could not move Beth right away. "Charles, please go with the other patients and staff down to the operating room. I'll move Beth out as soon as I can. Give me a little time to figure out what happened tonight during the assault and as soon as I have been assigned a location to move her to then I will come and get you. But, I want you to get out of here, now. It's not safe for you, and I can't have anything happen to you. I'll take care of Beth."

As quickly as the emergency room burst into fury from the bomb threat, it just as quickly fell eerily still. The emergency department suddenly was like a ghost town. All of the rooms were empty, and some of the cabinets remained open from the hurried exit of staff grabbing last minute supplies. The phone was quiet. The department was silent, except for a few squelches on police radios.

Beth, looking much younger than 20 years old, was 5'2', of medium build, with short brown hair in a pixie cut, large round brown eyes, olive-toned skin. Naturally attractive, she wore just enough makeup to accentuate her genuine beauty. Addie thought Beth must have looked really cute for her date with Charles, in her short pink dress and flats. Beth was quietly lying on the hospital stretcher, flat affect, no crying, no smile, utterly still. Her hair was slightly tousled; there was smeared mascara under both eyes.

Addie stood at the stretcher and leaned in looking at Beth, her green eyes were as serene and calming as her voice. "Hi, my name's Addie. I'm the forensic nurse that's been called in to collect evidence from the assault. I'm glad to take care of you tonight, but I am sorry for the circumstances. Please, feel free to ask questions during the evidence collection process. I do have to move quickly. I need to collect evidence fast because a bomb threat has been called into the emergency room and I am waiting to hear from the charge nurse to be given the location where we will be transferred to. I've already sent Charles to a safe area; it's too dangerous for him to be here if he doesn't have to be.

"I didn't want to waste valuable time in talking to Detective Knight first, so I will get the details from him once we are moved to a safe location. For now, and it will seem like I'm moving fast. I want to get your consent so then I can begin with the evidence collection." She showed Beth the consent form and read directly from it:

> *This consent form gives the named forensic nurse examiner permission to ask you about the assault details, obtain blood and urine samples, collect clothing worn during the assault and swab areas of your body that they feel may contain traces of evidence including DNA and debris. This consent includes photographs of your body, including your genitals. A genital exam will be performed, including a speculum exam, collecting vaginal swabs and taking vaginal and anal photographs. The sexual assault forensic exam will move at a pace that is most comfortable for you.*

Both Addie and Beth signed and dated the consent form.

Addie drew blood from Beth. The patrol officer looked away as Addie took the long straight needle, with an empty red top tube attached and pierced through the antecubital space of Beth's inner elbow. Blood flowed rapidly into the red tube; once filled, Addie filled two more tubes, one grey and one purple. The blood flooded, brimming inside the tubes, causing a layer of minuscule bubbles to float on top. Addie needed the grey top tube of blood in order to obtain a baseline of Beth's blood alcohol level. The red top tube of blood was to determine if Beth was pregnant, and the purple top to submit to the crime lab for a 'known' blood DNA sample. The officer continued to look away during the blood collection, unable to bear the large straight needle sticking out of Beth's arm. Beth then provided a urine sample to test for any drugs in her system, even though she denied ever using drugs. However, the boys might say Beth was using drugs with them; the sample would confirm who was telling the truth.

Addie was shaking from the threat of the bomb. With every cabinet she opened, she wondered if the movement of the cabinet door would detonate an explosion. When the phone began ringing, she jumped in fright. Her heart started racing; she was afraid to answer, but realized that she must suppress her fears. She had a job to do. By the fifth ring she answered the phone. What a relief to hear Madison calling to say that a recovery room was available. She opened the door; out in the ER, she saw police officers and the bomb dog, Violet, scanning the large department for the bomb. Addie quickly moved Beth on to a stretcher. Once in a private room in recovery, Beth slowly climbed off of the ER stretcher. Before taking a seat, she placed her purse on the white sheet that covered a gynecology surgery stretcher.

"I know that you told Detective Knight what happened. Go ahead and have a seat on the stretcher. I will need to ask you some questions and find out from you, in your own words, what happened. What can you tell me about tonight?" Addie rolled a black stool closer to Beth, so she could sit while they talked.

Beth spoke in a matter-of-fact manner. "Charles and I went to a party. I didn't know anyone there except for Charles. The house was really big and there were at least a hundred people or more. I was hanging out with a few girls in the kitchen and we were doing shots of Jameson and chasing it with ginger ale. I went outside to smoke a cigarette and I felt like everything hit me really fast. I realized that I drank too much, too fast."

Addie was documenting every detail that Beth recollected.

"There were three guys outside with me and one of them said to me: 'I've been watching you' and then they walked back inside the house. I stayed outside to finish my cigarette. After I put it out, I went into a bedroom on the first floor looking for Charles and there were the three guys. One of the guys walked out of the bedroom. The other two guys stayed, and started talking to me, they seemed nice and I didn't think anything of hanging out with them and talked to them for a bit."

Addie asked, "What were you talking about?"

"I don't remember, it was small talk, nothing important." Beth continued. "I was kinda upset that Charles brought me to this party and then went off with his friends. One of guys, he had reddish hair, closed the bedroom door. The dark brown-haired guy was the one who said "I've been watching you." They were doing shots and told me to do one, so I did. Soon after, I changed my mind about being there and thought that I should leave and so I casually walked over to the door. The shot that I had just done was kicking in and I felt a little off balance. Actually, I thought I was going to throw up.

"Suddenly, I didn't want to be in the room with them anymore. As I placed my hand on the door knob I felt scared. The guy, I think his name was Allen, the one with the dark brown hair, he followed me to the door and started kissing my neck. My heart was uncomfortably racing; I didn't want to be there. I didn't want to seem like a bitch so I tried to be polite and kinda pushed him away or maybe it was more of me turning away from him. I didn't want to be rude, I didn't want to make a big deal out of anything, I just wanted to leave.

"Allen forced me down onto my knees and dragged me, he forced himself in my face. Before I knew it, they had me on the bed."

"How did you get onto the bed?" asked Addie.

"I don't remember, everything seemed to happen so fast."

"What did you feel, or I guess, how did you feel?"

Beth shuddered. "I felt total panic, I no longer felt the alcohol, and I was instantly sober. My heart was pounding; I felt that his face was so clear. His brown hair, it was wavy, he had the straightest teeth, but they were big and made his face look wide. His jaw was wide and strong and defined. His eyes were blue but the center was large, round and dark. He kept staring down at me, expressionless.

"I was pinned down by the red head guy and Allen was on top of me pulling up my dress and was taking off his clothes." She was talking faster now. "I was flailing my body back and forth, trying to get my hands free. I kept telling him 'No, stop it.' Allen reached inside of a black backpack. He pulled out a gun. He laid it in on the floor. Then he pulled out a bottle of lotion. I froze in total fear. I couldn't move. I wanted to run. I wanted to scream. I thought about scratching him, but I could not move. The next thing I know, the red-headed guy was standing with his pants down; he had a condom on his penis."

Addie, "Was his penis erect, or hard? When did he put the condom on?"

Beth replied, "His penis was hard, erect, I mean. I think the condom was on his penis when he pulled his pants down because I didn't see him put it on. Before I walked to the door, he was in the bathroom; I think he put the condom on his penis when he was in the bathroom. I think he planned this."

"You're doing great," said Addie. "Just take your time and tell me what else you remember."

Beth answered, "I don't know. Everything was clear when I was at the door and when I realized something was wrong and I needed to get out of there, but after that it's just snap shots of them taking turns on top of me."

Addie spoke reassuringly, "If you can, I need specific details of what body parts came in contact with your body parts."

Beth choked back her tears, "The red head guy he was on top of me and I felt his penis go inside and he was thrusting really hard."

"What did you do?"

"I cried," she sobbed. "All I could do was cry! When he started pulling up my dress and pulling his pants down, I thought he would rape me, so I tried to push him off. When Allen pulled the gun out, I froze. I couldn't think anymore. I was just frozen with fear. I didn't want to be a bitch; I didn't want to make things worse. I tried to push them off, but once the gun came out I felt confused; I couldn't put two thoughts together. I couldn't save myself." She wailed. "Why didn't I hit them or scream or run out of the room? The door was right there!"

With her emotions vehemently swinging from one end of a pendulum to the other, Beth drew a deep breath. She slowly continued, in a flat calm voice, after another deep breath. "After Allen stopped, he then held me down and let the redhead rape me, too. Then when they were done, they got up and left like nothing happened. I was still crying and after a few minutes, I put my clothes on. I found Charles and told him I needed to go to the emergency room. He doesn't know exactly what his friends did."

Addie gently inquired, "You mentioned the lotion. Can you tell me anything you might remember about the lotion?"

Beth stared at the wall, thinking. "The smell, it was clean, like almond soap would smell. Allen had it in his hands. He tried to spit saliva in his hand and then rub his spit on me, on my vagina. But, the redhead gave him the lotion bottle. Allen pumped lotion into his hand and started rubbing his fingers and then rubbed it inside of me before he put a condom on and forced his penis inside me. I remembered it burned. He raped me, he used such force ramming himself in me, I couldn't get my breath, it hurt so bad."

"So Allen did not have a condom on already?"

Beth shook her head. "No. Just the redhead had the condom on before he pulled his pants down, not Allen."

Addie used firm but soothing tones. "I'm a little confused, and I understand the fear you were under makes it very difficult to recite the account in a timeline. I want to make sure I'm following you. Can you remember who put his penis in you first? Focus on what you saw and the smell of the lotion."

Beth calm and methodically recalled, "The redhead, who had the condom on his penis when he came out of the bathroom, raped me first. Allen put on a condom on when the redhead guy was raping me. I don't know why, but I was watching Allen the entire time. I didn't know what he was going to do. I was scared. Allen then got on top of me, forcing his…" She sighed a deep, sad sigh. "…His penis in me, he was really hard and very forceful, thrusting. It hurt. It hurt really bad. Allen then took the gun out of his backpack, while raping me. He pulled out of me and then held me down while the redhead guy raped me a second time."

Addie, "Where are the condoms, and did either of them ejaculate?"

Beth replied, staring at the wall. "I can smell the lotion. The condom fell off of the red head and I think he might have ejaculated on my dress. They threw the condoms in the trash. I don't remember seeing the redhead use a condom the second time he raped me." As she finished Beth looked at Addie with eyes full of naked, raw pain.

Addie stood up reaching for the crime camera on the counter, switching the camera's light "on" to shine a blue light, looking for body fluids. "Beth, I want to start the exam by shining a special light onto your clothing. I have to turn off the lights so the room will be dark. Put on these goggles, they're orange but they will protect your eyes from the blue light that I'll be using. I'm wearing similar orange goggles. But my orange goggles will filter the blue light so that I can see if there are any areas of fluorescence on your dress or body, which could indicate bodily fluids." Addie used the alternate light source and found a line of fluorescence that began glowing as soon as the blue light shone on the dress in the dark room, hoping it was semen from one of the boys. Snapping a few pictures under the blue light, Addie was able to photodocument the fluorescent stain on the pink dress. Turning the lights back on in the exam room, Addie continued the forensic exam. She filled out the forensic photocard, writing:

FORENSIC PHOTO DOCUMENTATION:
CC# 61-984-0263
Detective: Frank Knight
Forensic Nurse: Adeline Donovan, BSN, RN, FNE-A/P, SANE
Victim: Beth Walters
Charges: First degree rape, second degree sex offense.
Date and time: 0130 am, March 1, 2016.

After photographing the forensic identification card, she started photographing Beth's face and then Beth standing in the dress she was wearing during the assault. Capturing Beth at this particular horrible moment in time with her hair disheveled, make-up smeared, and stains on her dress to serve as the record of how she appeared in the emergency room.

Then Addie inquired," Was there oral involvement during the assault?"

Beth shook her head. "What do you mean?"

"Did they force their penis in your mouth? Did they put their mouth on your vagina?" asked Addie.

Beth nodded, laughing inappropriately for a few seconds. "Yes, Allen, he forced his penis in my mouth."

"What can you tell me about that?"

Beth stated, haltingly, "He held my head, by my hair. He was standing in front of me and he dragged me to my knees. This was all in the beginning…then he forced his penis into my mouth." She paused.

"Go on," urged Addie.

Beth closed her eyes. "He grabbed my face, squeezing my jaws open, forcing my mouth to open when he took his penis and rammed it into my mouth. He said, 'bitch' and started laughing. I had a hard time breathing, he was so forceful. I was trying to pull away, but he was too strong. His voice was demanding but he was laughing; it was an angry, sinister laugh."

Addie asked, "What did he say while he was forcing fellatio on you?"

Beth, tears streaming down her soft olive skin, gazed at the floor with the sadness of defeat, softly recounting: "He said, 'Bitch, fucking do it now or I'll beat you to death.'"

"You're doing great. I want to begin collecting your clothing. So, please take off your dress so I can collect it for evidence. Next, I need to collect your panties." She handed Beth a hospital gown to cover her naked body after collecting her dress, bra and panties.

Beth was fluctuating with emotion from laughter to hysterics. "I wish I had fought them off." She choked on her sobs. "I had no choice, I said, 'No.' I told them to stop!"

"I'm sorry this happened to you, Beth. But you're doing great. I want to collect swabs from inside of your mouth and around your lips as well. Would you be able to open your mouth, so I can look inside for bruising? Does your mouth or throat hurt?"

"Yes, under my tongue and the back of my mouth hurts really bad. It hurts to swallow and to move my tongue," said Beth, exhausted with emotion.

Addie examined the inside of her mouth. "The frenulum under your tongue seems to be lacerated. It looks like a fresh injury and it certainly looks painful." She documented on the body map that there was bruising and petechiae of the soft palate on the roof of the mouth. "Tell me exactly where are you having pain?"

Beth answered, "My mouth is sore and my vaginal area hurts a lot."

"What areas on your body came in contact with theirs?" Addie asked again. "Did they grab you, kiss, bite, or lick you anywhere?"

Beth's voice faded into a flat monochromatic tone, exhausted from both the assault and the examination. "The redhead licked me on my neck and left breast. I think he bit me. I remember my left breast suddenly hurting at the same time he was thrusting inside of me, which was also really painful. At the time, it was difficult for me to differentiate exactly where the pain was coming from. I hurt everywhere. I tried to push him away but the other one, Allen, was holding me down."

"Did they threaten you?"

Beth recounted: "Allen said, 'Don't forget that I'm watching you, I'll find you and hurt you if you tell anyone. I have friends at your school to watch you. If you tell anyone then I will tell Charles that you wanted to have sex with us. Why do you think we used the lotion, Beth? So we didn't leave evidence. Allen then slapped me across the face."

"He actually said that?"

"Yes," Beth sobbed.

"Interesting," Addie replied, while thinking to herself, "What an asshole." She went on with the exam. "I'm going to swab the left side of your neck and left breast." Collecting swabs of her neck and breast, Addie notices an oval shape injury to the left breast. She documented it for her report. The oval injury contained a top and bottom arch pattern in dark red and deep purple with possible teeth indentations noted. There was faint purple bruising on the inside of the injury indicating central ecchymosis which Addie noticed as she examined the injury more closely. The top and bottom arch patterned injury seemed to have indentations possibly from teeth crushing the skin, causing small crushing tears. The area was swollen and painful to touch. "I think he might have bitten you. I'm going to collect a few swabs of the bite injury." Gently rolling a wet swab followed by the rolling of a dry swab, focusing on the small tears in the skin she collected for potential DNA.

Beth nodded. "Yes, I think he may have bitten me, but I don't remember if he actually did. I don't know why, but I can't recall a lot of the details. Except the gun. I remember the gun. I thought Allen was going to kill me." Looking directly at Addie, she choked, "I thought Allen would shoot me. I remember that I was really scared."

Addie asked, "Did they threaten you with the gun, or did they just have it where you could see it?"

"The gun was on the floor. Allen would look at it then look at me. He did that a few times, looking at the gun then back at me, almost like he was thinking about what to do with it."

Through training in forensic evidence collection from living victims, Addie had been taught to remain emotionally neutral. Looking shocked or surprised could cause the patient to shut down and withhold valuable information, for fear of embarrassment. For Addie, trying to be supportive but not emotionally harmed herself, was quite challenging. While listening to the heinous details of the assault, Addie calmly stated: "I need to perform a vaginal exam but first I want to take a series of pictures of your breast and use a blue dye to help me visualize any small cuts in the skin."

Addie took a photograph capturing Beth's left arm and both

breasts, orienting the area of the body. Next she shot a photograph of only the left breast. With her gray scale ruler, she measured the oval bruised injury. Measuring circumferentially 360 degrees she made sure to capture the oval wound with proper measurement. A forensic odonatologist might be asked to review the photos by the prosecution or possibly by the defense counsel. Addie carefully and gently rolled a deep blue swab containing toluidine blue dye to confirm acute injury and highlight marks in the skin. After wiping the blue dye from the skin, linear dashes formed around the oval injury, popping out the detail. The dashes were highlighted in the bright blue color from the dye, confirming the patterned evidence was that of teeth marks.

To Beth, who was wearing only a hospital gown, she said: "I need you to lay down on the stretcher and I will pull out the stirrups." Addie was seated on a round stool at the end of the gynecology stretcher. She helped Beth put her feet in the cold metal stirrups and asked, "Please scoot all the way to the end of the stretcher, until you feel like you're going to fall off." Addie lifted the hospital gown exposing Beth. Beth began to cry, then shortly was sobbing and shaking. Her legs trembled uncontrollably while in the stirrups. Addie covered her by pulling the gown back down, giving her a moment to collect her thoughts.

Addie knew she had to help Beth through the next few minutes of evidence collection. She asked, "Would listening to music on your phone help?"

"Yes, I have a playlist of my favorites. You don't mind if I play music?" Once Beth felt able to continue, Addie lifted the hospital gown again, just as Beth's chosen song "Titanium" by Sia began to play.

Addie explained: "I am going to try and be very quick. I know this is difficult for you. I am taking a few pictures of your external genitalia. You are going to feel a swab; I need to roll it over your external genitalia. After retracting the labia, I need to take a few more photos, and collect a few more swabs. You're doing great." After placing the swabs upright in the drying stand in order to dry before packaging, Addie commented, "I need to apply a blue dye to your vaginal opening and take a few more pictures." After gently removing the toluidine dye a small, linear laceration shone brightly blue! The acute laceration was also confirmed by Beth's report of 8/10 pain and faint dried blood.

"Now I'm going to insert a speculum and collect a few swabs from inside of your vagina." Addie hoped that a forensic biologist at the crime lab may be able locate DNA on at least one of the swabs. She continued the delicate collection of evidence. Since Beth came right from the scene and had not eaten, showered or bathed, the chances of collecting DNA were greater. Beth wept while patiently enduring the invasive sexual assault evidence collection. Then quietly she started singing to her song playing in the background in order to soften the tenseness of the situation.

Covering Beth with a white hospital sheet, Addie helped Beth sit up. "I'm finished with the exam. You did great. Let's pick out a new outfit for you to go home in."

Addie rummaged through a closet full of clothes, and handed her a pair of black leggings and a grey sweatshirt. "We provide clothing for patients like you, who have had their clothes collected as evidence after a sexual assault."

As Beth dressed she talked to Addie. "I wish I had fought them off or ran or screamed or something!"

Addie sat on the black, rolling stool. "You know what I tell anyone that's been sexually assaulted, who feels the same way that you do? If you're here telling me what happened, then you did the right thing. Whatever you did, it was the right thing. Because you are here, you are alive." Beth rested upright on the stretcher, with her leg tucked under her bottom, contemplating Addie while she was talking, intently listening. "The mind has a wonderful way of protecting us for survival. Under normal circumstances the front part of our brain is functioning. This frontal part helps us with rational thought, problem solving, and it stores memories based on emotions. Memories are formed through emotions, both happy and sad. When you remember a particular event, know that the memory has an emotional significance. But Beth, remember you said when you were at the door, you remembered all of the events leading to that moment but as soon as you felt unsure of what they were doing, your brain sensed fear and the events became fuzzy. Chemicals were released and shut down your frontal brain, the part responsible for memory and rationalization. Actually, we—all of us—rely on habits during situations in which we might be in danger. We don't want to overreact when we feel uncomfortable so we rely on the habit of politeness, which sometimes works in excusing us from a dangerous situation. But when you have someone who intends to do bodily harm then your habits of politeness are useless. As soon as 'fear' kicks in, and the frontal part of your brain shuts down, another area of your brain takes over. This primitive area of your brain takes over, but only for your survival. When your brain is on 'fear' mode, you won't remember a nice time line or memory of the events because that area of your brain has been turned off to maintain your survival. Your rational thought for running away is also shut down in the frontal part of your brain. Your body freezes as an attempt to prevent you from being killed. Submission is what keeps animals alive in the wild. Submission kept you alive. So as long as you are able to sit here and talk to me, then you did everything your brain allowed you to do for survival." Beth took a deep cleansing breath, nodding in understanding of her actions and that she should not indulge in self-blame.

"Let me find Charles, I'm sure he wants to see you. Please, let's sign your discharge papers, you and I will both sign if you don't have any questions. The paperwork also has listed all of the medication I gave you at the end of the exam."

After Beth signed everything, Addie said: "I'll walk you over to talk with our victim advocate, Ms. Valerie Kelly. She will provide a list of contacts for follow-up counseling services, and go over safety planning. We want to keep you safe. Please follow up with counseling; it is important in the healing process. It was a pleasure meeting you, but I am sorry for the circumstances. Please take care."

Exhausted, Addie took a minute to pause looking around the messy exam room, cluttered with dirty linens on the stretcher and swab packaging and paperwork on the countertop. She collected her thoughts and emotions before she called Detective Knight to discuss her findings. She was consoled by the sound of his voice on the phone.

"SVU, this is Detective Knight."

"Hey, it's me"

"Well, hello, me. I'm happy to finally hear from you. They just announced over the radio an 'all clear' in the ER. The call was traced to a cell phone on the hospital premises. The phone belonged to a nurse in the OR. But she had left it in her locker and swore she had not made the call. And according to the OR staff, she was in surgery at the time the call was made. Plus it was a man's voice. So we have another puzzle to solve. I'm glad you are safe. I hated leaving you there."

Addie gave an exhausted sigh. "It was probably that Dr. Emory. I swear that man has it out for me. You know, lately I haven't been comfortable working in the office late at night. It never bothered me before. I don't know what it is. Anyway, I'm exhausted and those boys were pretty vicious to this girl. I want to write up my report and get the evidence packaged; it will be another three hours before I call for the crime lab to pick up the evidence. We can meet tomorrow to go over the report. I'm too tired to talk now. I need to get some rest to collect my thoughts. I'll be in touch."

"Okay, sorry your night is so long, no rush, we'll meet up sometime over the next few days."

Hours later, her seventeen page report finally finished, including a detailed body map of injuries, Addie called the Crime Lab.

"Police dispatch."

Addie stated, "Hi, this is Addie, I have a kit ready for crime lab pickup."

The dispatcher inquired, "What's the CC number?"

"61-984-0263"

"I'll send an officer over, thank you."

"Thanks!" Waiting for evidence pickup, Addie logged in the evidence, maintaining the chain of custody until the crime lab arrived. She secured the police evidence kit, containing the swabs and detailed report of the assault, and also secured the bags of clothing in an evidence cabinet. While locking the evidence cabinet, Addie was startled by the distinct metal on metal click of the unlocking of the hallway door.

Chapter Seven: Who Has Time For Gatchell's?

"There is nothing on this earth more to be prized than true friendship."—St. Thomas Aquinas

Addie jumped, but breathed a sigh of relief as soon as she saw who had entered. "Rachel, hi! God, you startled me. I couldn't imagine who would be coming through that door in the wee hours of the morning. I bet the sun's not even up yet. So, what are you doing here? Were you called in?"

"Hi, Addie." Rachel greeted her in an upbeat but serious voice. "Yeah, I got called in by the ER for a strangulation exam. I'm hoping to apply what I learned at the strangulation conference last month".

Addie nodded. "Oh, yes! Also, I reviewed your last few cases that you precepted with Bobbi and you're doing a great job. You're very thorough in your sexual assault cases. Bobbi is another excellent forensic nurse; we are lucky to have such a great team. So, what's the story with the strangulation?"

"A woman was strangled by her boyfriend. He picked her up and threw her against a dumpster, and then he strangled her. According to the patient, he's a known gang member, and has a history of beating and strangling her. A group of people were outside and witnessed it, but not one person tried to stop him from nearly killing her. I guess they didn't want to get involved."

"Where did this happen?" queried Addie.

"Motel 106 on the east side of I-95."

Addie sighed. "Sounds like another girl lucky to be alive. I'm going to go home, but do you need anything? If not, I'm going home."

Rachel kept talking. "Yeah, you get out of here, I'm good. I learned strangulation charting and alternate light source photography at the training last month. It's been a big help."

Addie picked up her handbag. "Bobbi has been a forensic nurse with us for a few years. She's one of our best. And for some crazy reason, Bobbi is always on call when the police need a suspect exam. So if you ever need assistance with a suspect exam, Bobbi is the lady to call! She is really good at strangulation exams, too. I'm sure she explained the difference in using the ALS for bruises versus for fluorescence of body fluids?"

Rachel washed her hands. "Yes, she really simplified the process for me. I use the ultraviolet light and yellow camera lens filter to see bruising under the skin, and blue light with the orange filter to locate fluorescence. The camera's ring light is so simple to use, just the flip a switch turns on the ultraviolet or blue light. I'm ready to do this case on my own. It's awesome how we can capture the absorption of light by the blood under the surface of the skin in photos as well, allowing us to identify the borders of the bruise for exact measurement. I have been a nurse for several years and a death investigator and never knew about ALS used in bruises."

"The ALS is great. Just remember, only document the ALS result if you can also see visible bruising on the skin under normal white light. You can call me if you need anything; no two cases are ever alike. But I have no doubt that you will do a great job with this case. We'll all have to catch up, you, me, Bobbi, Ashley and Lisa. We should meet for drinks one evening."

"It's funny how Sergeant Moran, well, Kate, lives in the same building as us," said Rachel. "We will have to have everyone over, or meet out in Fell's for drinks. Kate is the boss of my dear friend Margo. Do you know my friend Margo, Detective Margo Kim? She's one of the Special Victims Unit detectives."

Addie assented, "Yes I do. She's a good detective and really pleasant to work with. SVU has a good group of detectives."

Rachel paused, and then she burst out: "Addie, guess who called me tonight? It was David! He explained why he has been away! He was fighting wildfires in California. Those fires are the most dangerous kind to fight. The wind direction can change in an instant, trapping firefighters in a wall of flames! I'm just glad that he made it back uninjured. We're going out tomorrow night."

"Oh, my gosh, that's awesome. See, I knew he didn't fall off the face of the earth." Addie smiled. "I'm so happy for you, Rach. Congratulations!"

Addie went home. After a three hour nap, she showered and dressed to meet Frank outside of Police Headquarters. The temperature was finally in the upper 60's, so they decided to find a bench outside to talk privately about Beth Walters' case. Addie handed over a copy of the sexual assault forensic nurse examination report to him as she discussed the findings of her forensic exam.

"You are aware I usually do not see this much injury on my patients. Often we don't see any injury on sexual assault patients, but it doesn't mean an assault didn't happen," Addie told him. Frank, with his eyebrows raised, seemed ready to hear of all the injuries imposed on his victim. Addie continued, "Beth had bruises and petechiae in her mouth and throat. The frenulum under her tongue was lacerated. She had a possible bite mark to her left breast which, you know, bite marks don't stand up well in court, because they are so hard to prove. However, with the use of the toluidine, highlighting the teeth marks, our chances are good. Also, I swabbed the bite mark, so maybe we might get a DNA profile. Beth also had a small tear to the outside of her vagina, if you are looking at her vaginal opening, the tear, which was confirmed by toluidine blue dye, is at 6 o'clock, with redness from 4 o'clock to 8 o'clock. Looking at all of the injuries, they seem to corroborate her story."

Frank and Addie thoroughly read through the sixteen page report. Then she said, "I have to get back to the office for a meeting, feel free to call me if you have any questions, or call me if you don't have any questions." She smiled as she spoke.

Frank looked her directly in the eyes. "I was hoping I could take you to lunch?"

Addie stood up. "That sounds nice, but I can't do lunch, how about drinks later this week? Something simple, but nice. Umm, how about Gatchell's on Charles Street in Mount Vernon? I have plans to meet up with my best girlfriend Pam and her husband Jim. I haven't seen Pam in a while. But also Laura, Rachel and some of the other forensic nurses have also wanted to get together? Would you like to meet at Gatchell's, tomorrow night, say 6:00 pm? It will be a nice big group of us. Have you met Ashley and Lisa, the other forensic nurses that I work with?"

Frank replied, "Yes, I have met Ashley and Lisa. And of course, Laura, your boss. And yes, Gatchell's sounds good. I'm sure you all are a lively group. I'll see you then."

Addie hugged Frank, smiling a little as she walked away. When she reached her car, she glanced back; Frank was motionless, watching her. She waved and drove off.

Later that evening, Pam, Laura, Rachel and Addie engaged in group texting to plan their evening out on the town. Pam asked Addie, "Are we still meeting at Gatchell's tomorrow night? I haven't seen much of you since you and Cain broke up. We have to catch up"

Addie replied, "Yes! And Frank will be there too. I can't wait for you to meet him. I will invite Ashley, Bobbi and Lisa also, they are other forensic nurses I work with. You'll love them."

Pam texted in reply: "Perfect, Jim and I will see you tomorrow at 6."

Rachel responded, "See you at 6."

Addie and Frank arrived shortly before 6:00 pm. She was anxious to see him and he appeared equally anxious to see her. He waited as Addie parked her car. He approached her in the parking lot and she welcomed him with a hug and quick kiss on his cheek. From under her black leather coat wafted the scent of Roses de Chloé. She accepted his proffered arm and walked towards the restaurant. Gatchell's was one of Addie's favorite bars to have a drink and unwind. She was enchanted by the 1920's architecture and the art deco moulding around every doorway. Black marble surrounded a fireplace, highlighting an ornate white mantelpiece. White marble floors accentuated an art deco rosewood bar, which was where Addie and Frank sat. A grand brass chandelier floated above the patrons, illuminating enough to enhance one's good features. Once inside the bar, she removed her coat, exposing a crisp white t-shirt, and jeans. Over the intercom wafted the voice of Ella Fitzgerald crooning "Skylark."

> *Skylark, have you anything to say to me,*
> *Won't you tell me where my love can be?*

Seated very close to one another, Frank had his hand at the back of her bar stool. Addie ordered a whiskey sour. It was a delight to chat about their busy week. Ashley and her husband arrived, giving Addie a welcoming hug. Soon Lisa and Laura entered the bar, followed by Pam with her arm on Jim. Then Rachel arrived in a black knit dress and a couture black wool jacket, her curls flowing around her shoulders. She asked, "Where's Kate, Margo, and Bobbi?"

Addie reached over to hug Rachel. "They are working a case. Apparently someone is targeting young girls at bus stops."

Rachel raised her eyebrows in disbelief. "At bus stops? Are you serious?"

"Yeah, you can't make this stuff up!" replied Addie. "There have been two other girls who have reported being pulled into nearby woods and assaulted while waiting for the bus. We did a rape kit on one last week. Bobbi is doing the forensic exam after Detective Margo Kim, who is at the hospital now, finishes interviewing the victim. Sergeant Kate Moran is out at the crime scene." She paused, taking note of Rachel's chic attire. "Rach, are you meeting someone? Someone other than us, I mean?"

Rachel answered in breathless whisper, "Yes!" She tilted her head slightly in the direction where a tall, well-built man was standing by himself, against the backdrop of a Frank Lloyd Wright stained glass window, looking around for his date. "It's David! I'm meeting David!"

Addie's eyes widened as she mouthed the words: "Oh. My." Rachel, wearing black stilettos that matched her jacket, made her way over to the door where David awaited her. Addie saw him kiss her respectfully. He sported a pale blue pin-striped cotton shirt, open at the neck, and khaki trousers. She watched as Rachel and David made their way over to join them at the bar. Addie's excitement for her friend almost eclipsed her own joy at being with Frank. After ordering drinks, the friends took over a few cozy leather couches in a lounge area.

The couples enjoy their rare evening out, laughing and enjoying the downtime from their stressful jobs. They easily found solitude and relaxation in the company of friends, while sharing an abundance of appetizers. A night out, and the break from life, had been much needed.

Around 11 o'clock Addie called it a night and decided to head home. Frank offered to walk her to her car. She waved to Rachel and David. They waved back but then Rachel hurried over to her.

"Let's head for home," she said to Addie. "Tonight is my first night on call by myself."

Their friend Lisa, sipping her beer, quickly remarked, "Oh, Rachel, you'll do a great job!"

"How exciting!" exclaimed Laura. "Brandi's the charge nurse tonight, so if you need anything, she can be a big help to you. She has short stylish hair with a little streak of purple, and she's very pretty."

Addie's gaze swept over her friends. "Rachel, you'll be great. Oh, so that's why you drank iced tea tonight. Now I get it. Well, I testify in court as the forensic nurse expert. The trial starts in two weeks, and the victim is testifying first. I testify after the detectives, probably day two of trial. Could anyone meet next week to help me prepare?"

Rachel responded, "Even though I haven't testified yet, I can meet you next week. I can help you with whatever you need. I'll definitely attend the trial."

"You'll be great!" Lisa exclaimed, raising her beer.

Addie laughed at Lisa. "Thanks for the encouragement. You are all about the accolades tonight, Lisa. I love it!"

Lisa said, "Seriously, I can meet you next week also. I need to learn how to prep. I can't wait to watch you on the stand. Maybe we can go to lunch after?"

Ashley interrupted, "I'll meet you at the office and help you prepare for trial too. I have never testified and the thought of getting up on the stand terrifies me."

Pam laughed. "I would love to go, but I'd never get off from my job in the 9-5 computer world. I want to hear all about it." Addie gave her longtime best girlfriend a huge hug, "Thanks for coming out tonight, it was so great to see you and Jim."

Addie and Rachel gave each of their friends a hug and waved 'goodnight' to the group. "I can't wait to hear what happened with David!" Addie whispered to Rachel. Frank walked Addie to her car as David walked Rachel to hers. Frank, being a few inches taller than Addie at 5'9', placed his hands on her waist and leaned down to kiss her softly on her lips. She returned his kiss with a less subtle one, making future intentions perfectly clear.

"I'll call you," she told him. "The next two weeks I'm busy preparing for trial and I'm on-call almost every night." Sighing in her car, she wanted nothing more than to be with him.

Chapter Eight: Unfair Odds

"Everything can change at any moment, suddenly and forever." —
Paul Auster

Having dinner with Addie and Frank at Gatchell's that night had
been so much fun. Rachel was unable to sleep because of the random
thoughts racing through her mind. "Oh, I wish I could have had a
glass of wine. I can't believe I'm on call by myself for the first time
since obtaining my certification as a forensic nurse examiner."
Rachel's nerves kicked into high gear from repeating the steps of the
exam over and over in her head. After hours of worry, she fell sound
asleep.

Then the phone rang. Rachel jumped out of bed, awakening while
standing at the side of the bed with her phone in her hand. It was
automatic behavior; she had been in such a deep sleep that her mind
struggled to catch up with the person on the other end of the phone.
Peering at the clock next to the bed she saw that it was 3:21 am. As
she grabbed the pen and paper on the nightstand next to the bed,
Susan, the charge nurse, was already giving Rachel the name of the
patient, Mari Lu, who was waiting in the ER with the police. "Mari
Lu is in room 3 in the urgent care area of the emergency room with
police and Special Victims Unit Detective, Sergeant Kate Moran."

Nervous and excited, Rachel leaped out of bed, grabbing her
scrubs and pulling them over her riotous blond curls. She was glad

that her first case was with a detective she already knew. Rachel was comfortable working with Sergeant Moran.

Rachel arrived at the emergency room 40 minutes later, alerting the charge nurse, Susan, that she was there. She went to the secured Forensic Unit and grabbed an exam kit and the camera before popping into room 3. She smiled and nodded to the security guard, Jerry, as she passed him. Jerry's eyes were fixed on Rachel, as if his attention was heightened by why she was called in. "Hi Rachel. I hear you have a patient in room 3. Do you need anything?"

"No, but thanks." Rachel paused. She felt that she should be on alert but was unsure why. This was her first case and she was not letting anything, or anyone, get in her way of doing an excellent job. She shook her head and dismissed Jerry, going about her business.

Sergeant Moran had already completed her interview and was waiting for Rachel to arrive so she could provide her with the information she would need for the kit. She pulled Rachel aside before she entered the room, expressing concerns about Mari Lu's report of passing out. "There have been cases in the past that a victim did not know they had been sexually assaulted while they were unconscious. Could you please explain the importance of having a SAFE exam completed?"

Rachel responded, "Of course, I couldn't agree more."

It was hard for Rachel not to gasp in shock at the condition of her patient. Mari Lu's skin was a pale ivory color before three unknown men enticed her into their SUV to give her a ride home last night. When Rachel entered the room, all she saw was a young lady cowering in the corner of a stretcher. She had long, straight black hair which shielded the pain in her vacant eyes. As she pushed her hair aside for a moment, Rachel got a clearer look at the victim. Both of her eyes were swollen, with crimson bruises around them; her nose was also bruised and very swollen. The left side of her cheek and jaw were also swollen with a large, burgundy bruise beginning to appear. On the left side of her neck, three linear purple marks were surfacing from the trauma beneath. Rachel noticed that the right side of her neck had a single purple bruise on it. She realized that the bruising on Mari Lu's neck was a patterned injury that was consistent with manual strangulation. Rachel's concern for the girl, who was shielding her feelings by having her hair cover her face, was overwhelming. Rachel was convinced that Mari Lu may have been sexually assaulted as well. It was going to be one long night!

Rachel experienced heaviness in the room as she thought to herself, "Is this what I should expect to feel every time I come in for a case? How is it possible for human beings to do such horrible things to another human being?"

Rachel explained the exam to Mari Lu; the importance of doing a SAFE exam as well as a forensic strangulation exam. She obtained written consent for both exams.

"Nothing you did last night makes it okay for anyone to do this to you" were the first words out of Rachel's mouth as she tried to make sense of the brutality of the assault.

Mari Lu continued to cry while telling Rachel, "I shouldn't have had so much to drink. I should never have accepted a ride from strangers. I should have waited for my friends to be ready to leave."

With unshed tears in her eyes, Rachel replied, "This was not your fault. None of this is your fault."

After thoroughly explaining the exam to Mari Lu, she decided to do the exam in the emergency room, rather than taking Mari Lu to the Forensic Unit because of the severity of her injuries.

Mari Lu told Rachel that she was in a bar with three girlfriends. "It was a dive. Old, faded red wallpaper tried to conceal the film of dirt on the walls. The rank stench of stale cigarette smoke permeated throughout. I was annoyed the sticky floors would ruin the fresh soles of my new Frye boots. We had been drinking all day. I didn't want to drink anymore, I was tired."

Mari Lu continued. "Around 11:00 pm I called an online car service for a ride home and went outside to wait. An old navy-blue Chevy Blazer pulled up with three men inside, two in the front seat and one in the back seat. As they pulled up to the door I didn't notice any decals in the rear-view window, but I got in anyway. The two men in front appeared to be younger, maybe in their 20's. They both had on blue jeans with dark colored, long sleeve tee shirts. The driver had an earring in his left ear, a small gold colored ring. I think he had a tattoo on the left side of his neck. I'm not sure what it was, I got a glimpse of it before I got in the car. The man in the back looked like he was in his 40's, appearing much older than the men in the front seat. His yellow, crooked teeth were framed by his weathered face with deep-set wrinkles. He must have worked manual labor his entire life. He was wearing a cowboy hat, jeans, T-shirt and a jean jacket. I remember he had on brown boots that looked like work boots; they were dirty. He had a tattoo under his right eye in the shape of a teardrop."

In a low voice, Mari Lu continued: "I was leery about getting into the car. The driver said he was dropping the other two men off just four blocks from the bar. I made the biggest mistake of my life when I got into that car."

As Mari Lu spoke, Rachel noticed how raspy her voice sounded and how she constantly coughed as if she was trying to clear her throat, a common finding with victims of strangulation. Based on the abrasion Rachel saw under her chin, it was apparent that Mari Lu lowered her chin while being strangled in an attempt to protect her airway. The injuries made her appear older than her twenty-two years.

Mari Lu looked at Rachel and began to cry. "I feel short of breath, and it hurts so bad to swallow. I have such a horrible headache," Mari Lu constantly tried to clear her throat. Rachel noticed that Mari Lu's pants were wet and smelled like urine.

Sitting next to the stretcher, Rachel waited patiently for Mari Lu to speak again. "The driver drove about six blocks, and I asked where he was going. He still hadn't dropped off the other two men. He told me 'it's not much farther' and continued to drive. I was so sleepy that I must have dozed off for a few minutes. Suddenly, I realized there were no more houses in sight; we were surrounded by woods. When the car pulled into a small clearing, the man in the back tried to kiss me. I pulled away and he just punched me in my left eye. I panicked and tried to open the door but it was locked. I started screaming as loud as I could when the man in the front passenger seat turned around and punched me in my right eye. I realized this is it; this is where they rape and kill me because I was stupid enough to get into a car with three strange men. I really thought it was the ride I called for."

Mari Lu paused for a few seconds; again Rachel waited patiently for her to speak. "The driver climbed into the back seat and was trying to pull off my shirt. Panicking, I bit his hand as hard as I could. His face changed, he had the look of a demon, his eyebrows protruding from his forehead, creating deep furrows, anger causing the hair on his head to stand on end. His eyes became large pools of empty blackness as he grabbed my shirt and with vile energy easily ripped it in half, letting it fall off of my shoulders as I tried to grab it."

Mari Lu, drawing a deep, cleansing breath, began to speak faster.

"I was screaming, wildly kicking, lashing out with my arms, hitting anything I could come into contact with. The older man grabbed me by the neck with one hand and covered my mouth and nose with his other hand. I couldn't breathe. I knew I would never see my Mom and Dad again. I would never have the chance to get married or to have children. Suddenly, I began to fight back, digging my nails into the arms on my neck and face, trying to pry the man's fingers off of my neck. I knew this was it, this is how I die. I saw stars and everything went black. Suddenly, I realized that my pants were wet and the hands on my neck were not as tight. I gave a swift, strong kick with both legs. I heard a loud scream and realized that I could breathe again. I think my foot made contact with his balls. As I lay there gulping in air, I heard the older man tell the driver to head back. I guess the driver got out of the back seat at some point; I really don't remember. As they turned onto the road the older man in the back seat leaned across me, opened the door and shoved me out of the car. My bare back made contact with the hard asphalt. It's so sore." Appearing utterly drained, Mari Lu slumped back against the stretcher.

Rachel moved on to complete the strangulation exam. She began to ask routine questions, documenting Mari Lu's responses.

"What was the date and time of the assault?"

Mari Lu responded, "It happened today, around 12:30 am, in the morning."

Quickly glancing at her watch, Rachel realized that it is already 6:30 am, and the assault happened about six hours ago.

Rachel asked, "Who strangled you?"

Mari Lu stated, "The older man, wearing the cowboy hat. His English was broken, so I didn't know what he was saying. I didn't know what he wanted me to do."

"Can you tell me how he strangled you?" queried Rachel. "Did he use one hand, two hands, or did he use an object, like a rope or cord?"

Mari Lu answered, "He wrapped his right hand around my neck and squeezed hard."

Rachel asked, "Did he come from the front or from behind you?"

Mari Lu replied, "He strangled me from the front while holding his left hand over my mouth and nose. I couldn't breathe."

Rachel posed the usual question, "On a scale of zero to ten, with zero being no pressure and ten being the worst pressure imaginable, what number would you give to the amount of pressure you felt on your neck while being strangled?"

Mari Lu replied, "A ten."

Rachel inquired, "Did the man say anything while he was strangling you?"

Mari Lu nodded her head as she answered, "Yes, but he spoke such broken English, and some words were in Spanish. I didn't know what he was saying."

Rachel asked another question, "What did you think was going to happen? What caused the strangulation to stop?"

Mari Lu responded, "I thought I was going to die. He stopped when I was finally able to kick him in the balls."

Next, Rachel went through a list of symptoms. "I need to ask you questions to help me figure out the extent of the strangulation. I will need to know if you had any visual changes, hearing changes, headache or loss of consciousness."

"My vision was weird," Mari Lu told her. "I saw stars first and then everything went black. I have a horrible piercing pain all around my head. There is a period of time that I can't account for, I can't remember what happened. I realized that my underpants were torn, but I don't remember how it happened. At some point I realized that I urinated on myself but don't remember that happening either."

Rachel put her gloved hand over Mari Lu's hand that hung limply in her lap. "That can happen when someone is strangled. It's not unusual, and it's nothing to be embarrassed about."

Realizing Rachel was trying to reassure her, Mari Lu attempted a forlorn smile, after which she winced because of the pain it caused in her face and mouth.

Pausing while Mari Lu again drew several deep breaths, Rachel continued to ask Mari Lu about additional symptoms. "Did you have any voice changes? Does your voice sound different to you?"

Mari Lu responded, "My voice sounds very different and I'm coughing a lot. I couldn't breathe when it happened, and I still think I'm a little short of breath. I also have a lot of pain on both sides of my face and on both sides of my neck."

Rachel took a few minutes to document Mari Lu's facial and neck injuries on a body map, talking quietly while concentrating on the details. "There is bilateral swelling around both eyes. Bruises, purple and dark blue in color noted to both eyelids, extending to the lower eyelash line. Purple bruising with gross swelling is noted on the bridge of the nose, with deformity and pain (eight/ten). Left cheek and left jaw are swollen with a purple bruising. Most significantly, the left side of the neck has three linear purple bruises. It's common to see three marks with strangulation because the little finger is unable to apply enough force to cause a bruise. The right side of the neck contains a single purple bruise, and there it is, the thumb mark! Let me guess, 'Cowboy' is right handed."

Rachel helped Mari Lu undress and don the hospital gown. "I want you to get fully undressed so I can examine your body, including your genital area. I would like to take photographs of any injuries. We are concerned you may have been sexually assaulted while you were passed out, after you first got into the car. Or when you were unconscious after the strangulation."

The ultraviolet light shining on the fresh bruises to Mari Lu's neck distinctly showed Rachel the extent of the bruising caused by the pressure of 'Cowboy's' fingers compressing the delicate vessels of Mari Lu's neck.

Rachel said, "Mari Lu, just a little while longer and I can turn the lights back on, but I want to re-measure the bruises to your neck. I am now able to better identify the borders of the injuries."

Mari Lu asked, "How is that?"

Rachel replied, "Blood absorbs light, providing a contrast from the surrounding tissue. The ALS is one of the tools a Forensic Nurse Examiner can use to enhance the visibility of an injury that may be only faintly visible."

Next, Rachel started Mari Lu's SAFE exam, collecting swabs that could potentially identify her attackers. Rachel was appalled by the extent of the injury to Mari Lu's vaginal area, several lacerations to her hymen between three o'clock and eight o'clock, one of them a complete transection through the hymen at five o'clock.

Leaving the room, Rachel found Sergeant Moran and offered to obtain swabs of Mari Lu's neck for touch DNA since her attacker was a stranger. At Sergeant Moran's request Rachel returned to the room and quickly obtained the neck swabs. She then went to report her findings to the emergency room physician. Calmly, she stressed the urgency of the situation to the doctor. "Mari-Lu, the patient in room 3, she has survived a near-fatal strangulation, so I recommend that she has CTA of her neck. The Cat Scan with a contrast injection is necessary to evaluate her carotid arteries for injury."

Upon returning to the SAFE exam room, Rachel completed the

SAFE exam report and the forensic strangulation report. Using a body diagram, she documented all of Mari Lu's visible injuries. Interrupted by the ringing of the office phone on the wall, Rachel answered, "Forensics department. This is Rachel."

She heard the voice of Sergeant Moran. "Hey, it's Kate. What did you find on our girl? Any evidence that she was strangled?"

Rachel responded, "She has pretty clear injuries that are consistent with her account of the events. In addition to the multiple injuries on her face, petechiae are visible in Mari Lu's once white sclera of her eyes. She has a few bright red dots from broken vessels behind her ears, in her scalp, and on the roof of her mouth."

"Can you prove the petechiae, those small hemorrhages, are caused by the strangulation?" asked Kate.

Rachel answered, "They are consistent with strangulation but petechiae can be caused by childbirth, suffocation, violent coughing, violent vomiting, blunt force trauma or some disease processes. We know she didn't deliver a baby tonight, so we can rule that out. I think Mari Lu's petechiae were caused by pressure being applied to the neck, causing the jugular veins to become occluded and blocking the outflow of blood from the brain. If the carotid arteries were still pumping blood up into the brain while the jugular veins were blocked, the pressure will continue to build up in the blood vessels. Just like a balloon that has no more room for air pops when it is overinflated, blood vessels will burst when there is no more room for the blood to go. Those broken blood vessels are most commonly seen in the whites of the eyes; however, they can be seen anywhere above the point of compression in a person who has been strangled. Mari Lu's findings are classic evidence."

"Awesome, thanks," retorted Kate. "What about sexual assault? Any signs of that?"

"Yes, she had significant injuries to her hymen. She is quite sore and doesn't remember anything about the sexual assault. I hope I was able to collect DNA. Maybe it will help you catch those guys. They need to be stopped, they need to be put in jail for a long time in order to stop them from doing this to anyone else." Rachel inhaled and continued. "I'll have a report ready for you shortly. Talk to you soon."

Exhausted, Rachel packaged her evidence and made a copy of both reports for Sergeant Moran. She glanced at the clock on the wall in the exam room and was shocked to find that it was 9:00 am already. "No wonder I'm so tired. Where did the time go?" she said out loud, knowing full well that nobody was there to answer her question. Rachel called the Crime Lab to come and collect the kit from the secure evidence locker. Placing a copy of the report for Detective Moran in a yellow manila envelope, marked 'Confidential' on the front with red 'Evidence' tape securing the closure to drop off to Kate's apartment at Thames Point, one floor down from Rachel and Addie. While Rachel was sleeping, Detective Moran would continue the investigation of Mari Lu's assault, searching for the men who assaulted her.

Rachel returned to her apartment. She was unable to forget Mari Lu, sitting helplessly on the stretcher with her hair shielding her face, and the deep-pitted finger impressions on her neck. Eventually she fell into a deep sleep.

Rachel did not wake up until noon. She heard the persistent pitter-patter of the rain on the roof and windows of the apartment. It was Sunday. After taking a quick shower, she heard her phone ringing. It was David. He surprised her by saying, "Frank and I made plans to take Addie and you to a champagne brunch at the Four Seasons."

Rachel thought, "This is most unusual, but it sounds like fun, even on such a rainy day." Rachel put on a black skirt with a lacy black blouse from Chico's with leopard-print pumps and a black leather jacket. She went downstairs where David picked her up.

Rachel and David ran into Frank in the lobby of the Four Seasons hotel. Addie was already there, seated at a table overlooking the Baltimore harbor. Addie was wearing a pale blue silk suit with pearls and her hair in a French knot. Rain was pattering down onto the ground and sliding down the hotel windows. As if on cue, a server brought over four flutes of champagne. The sounds of jazz radiated through the dining area to the low hum of patrons conversing and occasional dishes clanking while waiters cleared the empty tables. The pressing of the keys of the piano vibrated harmoniously with the bellowing sounds from a trumpet and percussion from the drums to the delightfully husky voice of a lovely jazz singer. The soothing melodies compensated for Rachel's sobering case the night before.

Addie and David ordered Eggs Benedict while Rachel had an omelet and Frank had Belgian waffles with strawberries and cream. They sat there all afternoon, sipping French pressed coffee and delighting in a few champagne cherry mimosas in tall fluted glasses. It was the longest brunch any of them had ever enjoyed, as they talked about how to solve all of the problems in the world. Rachel was delighted that Frank and David had so much in common and so much to discuss.

Towards the end of the meal, after the men took care of the check, David turned to Rachel. Staring longingly into her eyes, David said, "The first time I saw you, in the midst of all the chaos, I knew I had just met someone special."

"I felt the same way," replied Rachel. "I look forward to getting to know just how special you are." And hand in hand they gazed out the window at the harbor, silvered by a curtain of rain, with fuchsia and burnished clouds aglow at the horizon.

Chapter Nine: Always Be Prepared

"Pro-tip: if you absolutely must speak in court, do not put air quotes around 'the law.' Judges don't like it." —*@lawyerthoughts*

Addie arrived at the office before Ashley and Rachel in order to get a head start in reviewing the photos for the trial. On her way in, she ran into Jerry, the security guard.

"Hello, Addie! Do you have a patient coming in? Let me know if I can help."

"Thanks, Jerry, but not today," Addie told him. "I'm just meeting with the other forensic nurses to prepare for a trial. It's thoughtful of you to ask, though." He nodded slightly and proceeded slowly down the hall, keys jingling from his belt.

Laura was in her office reviewing cases from the previous days.

"Good morning," called Addie, as she sat in a chair across from Laura's desk.

Laura replied, "Hey, have we been busy. We had seven cases over the last five days. I'm going to be out of town for the next few days, will you be available to assist in any major sex crimes that might come our way?"

Addie said, "Yeah, no problem."

"Okay, thanks," answered Laura. "I'll make sure all of the detectives with the sex crimes units have your cell and home phone numbers."

"I'm not sure how to ask this, Laura, without sounding accusatory, but of the last seven cases, how many did Jerry offer to help out in? And, I don't know, I just feel something is odd about him. Has anyone else mentioned him, his unusual interest in *our* patients?"

"No, not really. He is liked by the ER staff. I haven't heard anything negative about him."

"Okay. Maybe it's just me. You know when you're working late and these cases, God, they make you paranoid after a while. Everyone becomes a suspect." Addie laughed off her suspicions.

Minutes later the door made a loud unlocking sound, as Ashley and Rachel entered the forensic nursing department.

"Good morning, Rachel," sang Addie. "Hi, Ashley. I've already uploaded the photos on the computer. Let's start by looking at the injuries then we can look at the questions. I have a copy of the court questions. The prosecuting attorneys don't always stick to the questions; they never want us to sound scripted, so you really need to know what you're talking about. With the questions, at least you have an idea of what the state prosecutors will be asking. God only knows what the defense will ask."

Looking through at least forty photos of injuries, Addie outlined what she will need to remember for the trial. Addie stated, "Let's get started by reviewing the photos."

"Which case is this?" asked Rachel.

Addie replied while turning her chair toward Rachel and Ashley, "The patient's boyfriend came home after drinking all day and he was passed out on the couch. They had been living together for about a year. Arguments had been escalating. Police were called to respond to the apartment on numerous calls for domestic violence. This particular call was made after the violence escalated to the point where he stabbed and strangled her. Miraculously, she survived this vicious attack.

"The problem with domestic violence situations is that they are like a pressure cooker. An argument ensues, 911 is called, police arrive and diffuse the situation. Weeks to months later, violence in the house erupts again. With each violent episode in which police are called back to the scene, officers become familiar with the victim, the suspect and the location. It becomes another routine call for the officers. What officers sometimes don't realize is that the violence inside of the home is escalating. With each 911 call, the suspect is becoming more violent. This guy quickly increased his level of violence, almost killing his girlfriend by stabbing and strangling her. Suspects who kill police officers in the line of duty, commonly have a history of domestic violence, and often with strangulation as a component of the violence."

"It's interesting that you would point that out," commented Rachel, "because on the news yesterday, two officers were shot, one was killed, after responding to a call and the suspect has a history of domestic violence."

Laura glanced up from the paperwork on her desk and nodded. "Yeah, suspects who strangle their intimate partners...these are our cop killers."

"It is really sad that society actually has cop killers," agreed Addie. "By looking at the first ten pictures, this patient has a defense wound. The incisional wound measures 20 cm long, which is about eight inches, with the cut extending from her outer arm down to her wrist. She received sixteen stitches in the emergency room. See how she was protecting her face from the knife. Defensive wounds are usually found on the forearms, because the victim puts their hands up protecting their face and body. When you look closely at the knife wound, you can tell the directionality of the knife based on how the skin is shored or lifted away from the wound, causing a minute pile of skin to form. In this case, initially I thought the knife cut in the direction of her elbow to her wrist, but once I had her hold her arm in front of her face and I closely examined which way the skin was lifted. I could clearly identify that the knife cut her from the wrist down toward the elbow. Her hand was up, with her palm facing and protecting her face. Her boyfriend slashed her arm in a downward motion. Classic defense wound."

Ashley asked, "Why not just call it a laceration? Why call it a cut or incisional wound?"

Addie scrolled back to the knife wound on the arm, explaining: "Any injury from a knife, blade, glass or other sharp object is a cut. Or an incision. Lacerations are caused by blunt force trauma, not sharp objects." Addie displayed the next grouping of pictures on the large computer screen. "Rachel, tell me what you see in this picture?"

Rachel answered, "Well, she has a broken front tooth with lacerations and bruising inside her mouth. No external bruising is visible. I would say her injury is caused by blunt force trauma to the face. Did she report him punching or hitting her in the face with fists or an object?"

"Yes," said Addie. "She told me that she thought he punched her in the face, but she could not recall how many times and has no solid memory of him punching her. She remembers having a bloody nose but does not remember being hit specifically in the nose. She really lacked a timeline and her story was quite fragmented when it came to her facial injuries. Her narrative was consistent with what we know about memory during trauma. Her best memories were about when he tried to kill her with the knife and strangle her, because fear was at the highest. She super-encoded those two events. The details are very specific surrounding the knife slashing and strangulation."

Rachel and Ashley looked through the next several photos of the strangulation on the computer screen. Ashley commented, "Oh, the marks on her neck."

Addie nodded. "Yeah, ligature marks from the belt were visible on her neck during my exam. You can clearly see, in the photos, the patterned mark was most likely caused from the belt stitching. The thick stitching caused the linear dotted pattern around her neck."

Rachel queried, "Did the crime lab find the belt at the crime scene?"

Addie responded, "Yes, they have the belt and it belongs to the suspect. It was leather with stitching along the edge. Moving on through the pictures, she has bruising to her left chest and left arm. She does not recall if he punched or stomped her."

Rachel sighed. "What on earth were they fighting about?"

"Was this the case in which they were fighting over a cell phone?" asked Ashley. "She couldn't find it and then he exploded accusing her of cheating?"

Addie answered, "Yes, she asked him, while he was on the sofa taking a nap at 3 o'clock in the afternoon, because he started drinking at 10 am, if he knew where her cell phone was. He jumped up off of the sofa, she retreated into the kitchen. He followed her into the kitchen and she said he was screaming nonsense about how she's cheating on him. She said they argue and fight weekly. Police have been called numerous times; once they respond, she backs down. She has never had him charged for any of the assaults. She protects him. He has previously punched and slapped her and has threatened to strangle her, but never did, not until today. Today his threats came to fruition and he nearly killed her."

Addie paused a moment then went on. "Oh, here are the vaginal photos. She thinks he used an object to assault her, but she doesn't remember the details. She has fragmented memories of vaginal pain with him on top of her. He had his hands around her neck strangling her. Fighting to breathe, she only remembered the look on his face, being 'demonic and soulless' not the sexual assault. On this picture, we clearly see vaginal trauma. There is a laceration to the vaginal opening. I called Detective Knight with my thoughts of an object being used. He was at the apartment and had the crime lab collect beer bottles that were found on the floor in the kitchen. So if DNA was on one of the bottles it will come out in trial."

Laura commented to Rachel, "We usually don't know the result of our DNA before trial."

After examining all of the forensic photos, Addie opened her report on the computer.

"Addie, your charting is good; it reflects your photos," said Rachel. "In your final narrative you state, 'Patient is released to law enforcement with a sutured forearm incisional wound (cut), broken tooth, mouth laceration, broken nose, chest contusions, and report of possible sexual assault.' So, she was released with police?"

Addie said, "Yes, she was released with police. The assault took place in her apartment and police warned her that her boyfriend had not been arrested yet and he was on the run. They took her back to her apartment so she could get clothes and then the officer took her to her parents' house, where she would be safe."

"Let's go over some questions you'll be asked during trial," suggested Ashley. "At the end, we can come up with questions the defense might ask, which is always fun. Rachel, here are the questions so why don't you ask them to Addie."

Rachel took the paper with the questions and cleared her throat. "Please tell the court your name."

"Adeline Donovan." Addie batted her eyes in reply, chuckling to herself.

"Where are you currently employed?"

"Kings Valley Medical Center," Addie confidently answered, in a more serious tone.

Rachel asked, "How long have you been employed there?"

"3 years."

"What is your position?"

Addie proclaimed, "Forensic nurse examiner."

"How long have you been a forensic nurse?"

"3 years."

Rachel asked, "What does the term SAFE stand for?"

"Sexual Assault Forensic Examination."

"Could you tell us about your education and experience?"

Addie responded, "Yes, I graduated from Johns Hopkins University with a bachelor's in science of nursing and passed the board exam to become a registered nurse. I began working at Trauma One Regional Center and after two years became a forensic nurse examiner. I began working at Kings Valley Medical Center three years ago, which is where I'm currently employed. I have been a registered nurse for five years."

"What training have you received for your role as a forensic nurse?"

Addie replied, "I completed the forensic nurse examiners coursework and training. I attend annual training conferences in sexual assault and strangulation through forensic nursing agencies and the police departments throughout the country."

"Have you testified in court before?"

"Yes."

Rachel asked, "How many times have you testified in court?"

Addie said, "Five"

"Have you been declared an expert witness in court before?"

"Yes," affirmed Addie.

Addie explained to Rachel and Ashley, "If you are asked 'yes or no' questions, then you only answer 'yes' or 'no.' Don't go on and provide ANYTHING that the prosecution or defense did not ask. So, you have to carefully listen to each question and exactly what the question is asking. After you are asked a lot of questions about your forensic experience and education, they move to either a fact witness or enter you as an expert."

Laura added, "The prosecution will then ask the judge, 'Your honor, we move to declare the forensic nurse an expert in sexual assault and strangulation.' If the judge agrees that you have had enough training and the defense also agrees, then you will be moved to be an expert witness. This is when you, 'to a certain degree of medical certainty,' can render an opinion. If you are not deemed an expert witness by the judge then you will be moved to be a fact witness, only stating the facts in your report, offering no opinion in forensics."

Rachel posed the next question, "Were you working on the night the victim arrived in the emergency department requesting a sexual assault forensic exam?"

Addie sighed, "Oh that's right, I need to know the time of the assault. When the call was placed to 911. When the patient arrived in the emergency department. When I arrived and when I began the forensic exam. Basically, I need to know every detail of this sixteen page report. I certainly have my work cut out for me."

Ashley said, "The prosecution may ask you, 'Can you tell me what the victim told you?'"

Addie eagerly sat up straight. "In the patient's account of the event, she or he may talk in jagged, fragmented sentences. Which is why you should always document in the patient's words. It's not our position to clean up language for the jury or to make sense of the assault. Gather your evidence without expectation of what you will find. We document what we see and what the patient tells us, we stay in the middle of the road, we don't take sides, we present the evidence we collect. Remember that, too, so when you are up for trial, you will do just fine in court."

Rachel said, "So read from your report what the patient told you."

Addie read, "The patient stated, 'I was face down, he tied my hands behind my back, he took off his belt. Tied it around my neck, he dragged me into the bedroom closet. He cut me. I tried to block it. I was cut. The belt was through the silver part. I got my hands loose. I tried to unhook the belt. It was tight on my neck. I struggled on the floor. He was laughing. He kept beating me, my nose was bleeding. I guess he was beating me in the face. I ran out from the closet, across the bedroom, and tried to jump out of the window. He kept raging.'"

Laura interrupted. "Don't worry that you have a jagged, blunted story with the use of simple words, lack of timeline, lack of the details of the sexual assault when she was 'face down, he tied my hands behind my back.' Addie noted in her report that 'upon further questioning for clarification about vaginal and penile penetration, the patient reported that when her hands were tied behind her back was when the sexual assault occurred, unsure if it was penile or an object'. When someone is the victim of a horrible assault and have fear, they lose the ability to remember details in a timeline. This is normal account of events under 'fear'."

Addie continued, "I asked her to clarify details, during the strangulation exam. She was able to clarify, to quote: 'The belt was put around my neck and secured through the silver part.' I asked her what the 'silver part' was and she told me it was the buckle. She tried to jump out of the window."

"The eighth story window!" exclaimed Ashley.

Rachel asked, "'He kept raging.' What does that mean?"

Addie shook her head. "He kept the fight going. She tried to diffuse the situation but he kept fighting with her. The entire ordeal lasted five hours! Can you imagine? Someone 'raging' on you...yelling and beating, strangling then slashing you with a knife, for over five hours? I asked the patient, 'What can't you forget about the assault.' She clearly told me." Addie flipped through the report. "Here it is, written in my report, 'when I was in the closet, it was when the belt was around my neck and he was slashing me with the knife.'"

Ashley frowned, while pulling her hair back to put her heavy purse strap on her shoulder, "That's so sad. She endured hours of assault but her memory is when she felt the *most fear*. She must have been terrified."

Addie scooted closer to the computer screen. "Okay, I'm going to look over the photos of the injury again. Rachel, will you look at the injuries again with me? And I guess I will spend the rest of the day going over my report piece by piece. I have to pick up my suit from the laundry mat. I will see you ladies tomorrow at the courthouse. Trial starts at 9:30 am. Thank you so much for helping me. I will be ready."

Laura laughed. "Oh, and the defense...what a special breed of people they are. They seem to love black and white wide pinstripe suits. And usually there is at least one huge gold gaudy ring."

Addie smiled. "Although, I did meet, once, and only once, a rare defense attorney that was compassionate and sympathetic to the victim during trial. He was still able to defend the suspect, but with grace and respect for the victim and her family. I was shocked. I didn't know a compassionate defense attorney existed. But most defense attorneys are not so nice. It all depends."

Ashley, with her hand on the door to leave, turned and put her purse down. She looked at Rachel and said, "Be prepared for the defense to talk loudly and yell at you. I once had a defense attorney throw his arms up in the air in exclamation and then folded his arms as he brought them down from the air and put his head on the table, like a three year old having a temper tantrum, during my testimony. It was all a ploy to throw me off my game. Ignore it! The judge and prosecution will allow the defense to have temper tantrums."

Addie, in eager support, added, "Yes. It shows you know more than they do, and the defense attorneys don't like it. They feel intimidated and so their childish rants are a means to divert the jury's attention off of you. The defense does this nonsense so that the jury doesn't hear your expert testimony. Stay in the middle of the road. We do not work for the prosecution or the defense. So, I'm not sure why defense attorneys can be so callous toward forensic nurses. We call it how we see it. Stick to the facts and the chips will fall where they may. Unfortunately, it sometimes turns into a real shit show."

Ashley asked, "What are some questions you've been asked by the defense?"

Laura replied, "'Could genital injuries be caused by the application of the toluidine blue dye? I know this is a 'yes or no' question.' The mere suggestion of injury caused by rolling a cotton swab was so ridiculous, I just had to expound on my answer. I responded by saying, 'With a cotton swab? The injury was visible before I rolled the blue dye on with a cotton swab. No, I did not cause a laceration rolling a cotton swab across skin.'"

Addie put in, "Oh, my favorite, was when I was asked: 'How many cases have you worked with the defense? Let me ask it this way, how many times have you worked with the Dark Side?' Oh, my God! I wanted to burst out laughing! 'The dark side?' Are you kidding me? He was so sleazy. Then he asked me, he said, 'So, let me get this straight, you have completed 100 sexual assault exams but you have only testified 5 times. How can you explain that?' I thought, are you kidding me? You're really asking me that? So, under oath I answered his really stupid question. 'Yes, I have done 100 cases and only testified 5 times because the other 95 cases took the plea deal.' Oh my God, the expression on his face of complete shock and embarrassment with his eyes exclaiming out of his head, his face was instantly flushed, he was so mad he could barely let out his next question. Actually, that was his last question. He looked at the judge in disbelief, and she told him, 'You asked the question and you got the answer.' So, just answer the question however you seem best because you're under oath. Even I didn't want to answer his question, knowing how completely idiotic it was, but I still had to. Seriously though, thank you both so much for helping prepare for trial. I will spend the rest of the day going over the report and photos and will see you ladies at the courthouse tomorrow."

"I'll catch up with you at home," said Rachel. "But you will be great. I can ask you the questions again tonight and help for review."

"Thanks Rachel," replied Addie. "I'll be home later this afternoon. Laura and Ashley, thank you so much."

Laura asserted: "You know the case and the forensics, you'll be great and we'll all be there as your support."

The day of trial, while at the courthouse, Addie was sequestered until it was her time to testify. Rachel, Ashley, and Laura were sitting in the pews of the courtroom watching the prosecution and defense make their arguments and candor back and forth at the offering of a plea deal. A mahogany wooden railing separated the three ladies from the prosecution and defense tables. Aside with the forensic nurses, the benches were filled with friends and family of both the victim and the suspect. Instead of the families gathering for a wedding they had gathered for an attempted murder trial. No reception to follow. One lone reporter was sitting by herself, scribbling notes and sketches on a notepad.

By Wednesday afternoon the defense finally spoke on behalf of his client, "Your honor, through much deliberation and examining the surmountable evidence collected by police and forensics, my client has decided to accept the plea deal offered by the state of 15 years with 8 years suspended and mandatory life registration on the sex offenders registry."

The victim displayed great relief that she did not have to testify against the defendant. By throwing her hands in the air with joy and crying out loud while hugging her parents and sister, they were all satisfied of the plea deal. Addie and her forensic nurses were happy that the suspect admitted to his heinous crimes of strangulation, physical assault and sexual assault against his girlfriend, and would be facing a lengthy jail sentence of 8 years.

Rachel asked Addie, as they were leaving the courthouse. "What does all that mean, 15 years with 8 years suspended?"

"It means he will serve 8 years in jail, without the possibility of parole. The rest of the 7 year sentence, he will be on probation and if he gets arrested for anything he will automatically serve the remaining 7 years. For life, he will have to register as a sex offender. Either way, we all win and most of all she..." Addie nodded over to her patient, happy in the joy of the outcome. "...Doesn't have to take the stand and face him ever again." Addie went on to explain to Rachel, "You will prepare for one hundred trials and ninety of them will take the plea deal on the first day of trial."

Laura added, "But you always have to prepare, you never know which case will be the one that will move forward to a jury trial."

Chapter Ten: It Made Me Sin

"The weak can never forgive. Forgiveness is the attribute of the strong." —Mahatma Gandhi

It was a brisk winter morning. Rachel gave Addie a hug as they crossed paths in the kitchen. Addie was coming in to get some sleep after being called in for a case at one o'clock in the morning. It was now 5:45 am and Rachel was leaving for work. Her car seemed to be on auto-pilot as her mind wandered on the forty-minute drive to the hospital.

Rachel's thoughts drifted to David and the most amazing last few months of her life. She remembered their dinner the previous night, sitting across the table from him. They ate pizza and drank wine, talking about their life journeys, which had perambulated along parallel roads before finally intersecting so they could find each other. "My fireman," Rachel whispered. "I fell in love with him the minute he walked into the ER. I never knew that I could fall in love so fast and hard. David is kind and considerate, so sensitive to my feelings, and incredibly easy on the eyes. As well as looking really sexy in his firefighter's gear." Wrenching herself away from the images of him that played in her mind, Rachel realized that she was almost at the hospital.

As she pulled into the parking lot, Rachel murmured to herself,

"Here we go again, another day of chaos in the ER." She was assigned to triage, "to sort" the emergent from the non-urgent patients. Her desk was located in the front of the emergency room where patients first presented with their chief complaints. The triage nurse had the task of assessing patients and assigning an acuity level based on their complaints and the patient's level of stability. They also kept the charge nurse, who remains in the back, running the busy ER department, updated on patients waiting for the next room. Depending on their acuity, the charge nurse decided who received the next available room.

It was the triage nurse who was verbally assaulted on a daily basis by the patients with low acuity complaints, those who had to wait as the patients with the more life-threatening conditions were taken to a room before them. That said, Rachel loved triage. It took an experienced nurse to accurately assess and triage patients. Constant reassessment of patients was required to keep all of the patients in the waiting room safe, preventing negative outcomes.

It was a normal day in triage. Rachel walked in to a three-hour wait for a patient in the waiting room to get a room in the ER treatment area. Seeing a new nurse come in, patients began approaching the desk, asking how long it would be before they were taken back to a room. The constant influx of people walking through the ER door to be seen never slowed down. Working with an ER tech, Rachel calmly examined each patient, quickly assessing them and assigning an acuity level.

Rachel finally had everyone in the waiting area triaged. She stood at the registration desk, scanning the room, looking at each patient. She evaluated each patient for any possible sign that their condition has increased in severity. Rachel's scrutiny fastened on a man sitting directly across from her in the waiting room. Her gut instinct told her to reassess him. When he was triaged two hours earlier, he complained of sudden onset nausea and temporary left arm pain, which was resolved. His EKG and his blood work were negative.

Rachel left her triage area and walked over to the man. His skin glistened with moisture. He was not so much sweaty as he was clammy and cold when she touched him. "Sir, how are you feeling?" she asked.

The man gasped, "I have really bad left arm pain, and my chest doesn't hurt, but it feels heavy."

Rachel grabbed a wheelchair and quickly helped him into it. She quickly called the treatment area and spoke with the charge nurse, Andy. "Andy, I need a room for this man immediately! He's been sitting in the waiting area and had a normal electrocardiogram (EKG) on arrival, but he suddenly looks really bad. I think he's having a heart attack."

Andy replied, "Okay, we discharged the patient in room 14. We just have to clean the stretcher but it will be ready by the time you bring him back. I'll call for a STAT EKG.

Rachel helped the man out of the wheelchair and onto the stretcher, saying, "Sir, I need you to take off your shirt and pants. After assisting the man in the quick removal of his shirt and pants, she said, "I need to put you on the heart monitor then I can help you with your gown; it opens in the back."

The nurse assigned to the room came in with the EKG machine and hooked him up to the twelve leads. The EKG showed an anterior myocardial infarction.

The overhead intercom blared, "Triage to the front please. Triage to the front." Rachel left the room to see what the emergency was at the front of the ER. As she was walking down the hall she heard: "I need a doctor and a crash cart to room 14 STAT!" Rachel ran back to room 14 and saw the man to whom she had just been talking a few moments ago in full cardiac arrest. Overhead, she heard the frantic summons: "Triage to the front! STAT."

"Triage to the front!"

Rachel hurried to the triage area to find a fifteen-year-old teenager in a loose-fitting dress sitting in a wheelchair at her desk. Rachel asked her the routine questions: "What's your name, date of birth and what brings you to the ER."

Arms gripping the arms of the wheelchair, the teenager responded, "My—stomach— hurts."

Rachel took her into a separate room off of triage where they have more privacy and asked, "Is there any chance you could be pregnant?"

The girl responded quietly so her mother, standing outside of the room, did not hear: "No."

Doubting the truth of the teenager's response, Rachel ordered blood work and gave the girl a cup for a urine specimen so she could run a pregnancy test. The young girl stood up, walking to the bathroom, as Rachel carefully watched her, scanning for a sign of pregnancy. The girl was tall for her age, and her flowing dress so pregnancy. The girl was tall for her age, and her flowing dress so loose that a pregnancy could easily be concealed. Before the urine specimen was obtained, the teenager's mother rushed up to Rachel's desk, stating, "My daughter just urinated on herself. It's running down her legs. I couldn't get her out of the bathroom."

Rachel quickly called the charge nurse again asking for a room immediately. "Andy! Shit, her water just broke! I have a teenager, I think she's pregnant and her water just broke. I need a room!"

"Bring her back to room 5. It's clean and ready. You caught me just before I pulled another patient for that room. I'll call OB/GYN," Andy replied.

Rachel whispered into the phone, "She denies being pregnant, so I know she didn't have prenatal care." As Rachel wheeled the teenager to room 5 she whispered, "I think it's time for you to have a talk with your mom."

By noon the wait was up to four hours just to be placed in a room; it was several more hours before patients were seen by an ER doctor. The tension in the waiting room was palpable; patience was wearing thin. Rachel contemplated taking her lunch break when a disheveled man in his 30's approached her desk, plopping himself into the chair. She asked her usual questions, "What is your name and date of birth. What brings you to the ER?"

The man quietly responded, "My name is Tommy, I was born on November 10, 1988. I'm here because I cut off my penis." In the many years Rachel had worked in triage she had heard a variety of complaints told by patients in order to get to a bed faster. However, this was a new one to her. The man's flat affect, coupled with the fact that he wouldn't make eye contact with her, made alarm bells go off in Rachel's head. As an experienced nurse, she had learned to trust her gut, and Rachel's gut instinct told her that this man was seriously troubled. As she leaned over to put a blood pressure cuff on Tommy's arm, she spotted a puddle of bright, red blood accumulating on the floor beneath his feet. Rachel quickly motioned for Jerry, the security guard, to bring a wheelchair over to the triage desk, muttering to herself, "Damn, he's not kidding."

Rachel quickly placed Tommy in a wheelchair and rushed him back to the trauma room where they quickly realized that he really was telling the truth. Pulling his arms out of his coat as Tommy stood to get on the stretcher, Rachel laid him down and rapidly cut off Tommy's navy blue, blood saturated sweatpants and his gray sweatshirt. Rachel put two IVs in his right forearm and drew several tubes of blood to send to the lab. Concerned about the amount of blood Tommy lost, she connected a bag of fluids to each of the IV lines.

Rachel asked, "Do you have any history of psychiatric illness? Depression? How about a history of drug or alcohol abuse?" As she quickly placed monitor electrodes on his pale, clammy, hairy chest to monitor his heart rate she continued, "Why did you do this?"

Giving her a troubled look, Tommy replied "It made me sin."

"What did you use to make the cuts?"

In a muffled voice Tommy replied, "I started with a knife, but it didn't work too well. I finished with a razor blade."

Rachel listened to the heart monitor beep as she worked. Tommy's heart rate was 120 beats per minute and his blood pressure is 80/50. Rachel proceeded to start a third IV. She called the lab and requested several units of blood as soon as the type and crossmatch was completed. Next, she began to complete an operating room checklist, preparing Tommy for surgery.

The ER clerk called Dr. Dinkin, the urologist on call. He promptly responded to the emergency room to evaluate Tommy as the ER staff continued to prepare Tommy for surgery. By the time Tommy went to the operating room the police were able to locate the rest of his penis in his apartment and brought it to the ER. The urologist was able to reattach it. Tommy was admitted to the hospital on 24/7 suicide watch. He was not left alone for a minute, for fear he would cut it off again.

Police were back at the apartment looking at Tommy's computer. He was arrested and charged with operating a child pornography site. A police officer was posted at the door to Tommy's hospital room. Upon discharge from the hospital, Tommy would be taken directly to jail.

Rachel was finally able to take a fifteen minute lunch break. She barely swallowed her sandwich when she heard a panicked voice paging, "Triage to the front! STAT. Triage to the front!" Rachel dashed to triage to find Jerry the security guard and Kristi, the nurse who relieved her for lunch, trying to pick up a man in his 20's to put him on a stretcher. As Rachel helped them with the task, she noticed that both the front and the back of the man's tee shirt were covered with blood; he was unresponsive but still breathing. It looked like he had multiple gunshot wounds (GSWs) to his chest.

As they quickly ran the stretcher back to the trauma room, Kristi uttered in disbelief, "A black SUV with tinted windows pulled up out front. I saw the rear passenger door fly open. It looked like someone in the back seat pushed this man out of the SUV. Then the vehicle took off, I don't think it even stopped."

Knowing she had a line of patients at the triage desk, Rachel left the trauma patient in the competent hands of the ER treatment area staff and returned to her assigned area. When the police walked in looking for the patient who was shot, Rachel directed them to the trauma room.

Walking into the waiting room Rachel immediately noticed an elderly man lying on his right side on the floor with his right arm underneath his head, using it for a pillow. As Rachel walked up to the man, she noticed that he looked older than he probably was. He was wearing multiple layers of clothing, but he didn't have a winter coat on. "He probably hasn't had a bath in quite a while," Rachel mumbled as she got close enough to get a whiff of his body odor. She noticed that his shoes had holes in them. As he rolled onto his back and Rachel knelt down next to him, she also identified the strong odor of alcohol on his breath.

"What's your name?" Rachel asked.

"My name ish Phil," he slurred in response.

"What brought you here today? Does anything hurt you?" Rachel asked.

"My head and my hip hurt from when I fell today. I was at the liquor store down there," Phil responded as he flung his arm out, pointing towards the right.

After helping Phil into a wheelchair and getting enough information to quickly register him, she called, "It's Rachel in triage. Can I speak to Andy, the charge nurse?"

The ER secretary replied, "Charge is busy with another critical patient."

"Okay, tell her I'm bringing back a possible head bleed."

"Andy said to put him in room 2."

Rachel rushed him back, thinking, "Are his symptoms simply the result of being intoxicated or did he have a head injury or a head bleed from the fall?" She knew he would need a thorough evaluation, including a cat scan of his head, to make sure he was okay.

After helping him onto the stretcher, Rachel put up the side rails so he would not fall again. She located the nurse assigned to room 2, Samantha, so she could give her a brief report. Rachel was aware that Samantha had recently come from orientation.

"The man I just put in room 2 has been drinking today. His speech is very slurred." As Rachel continued, she noticed Samantha's not so subtle eye roll. "He told me that he fell this morning, hitting his head on the sidewalk." Aware that Samantha was relatively new to working in the ER, Rachel stated, "We need to make sure that his symptoms are from being intoxicated and not from bleeding into his brain."

"Well, yeah, I get it! He's drunk," barked Samantha

Knowing it was still busy out front, Rachel rushed back to triage. Pausing at the door to room 2 she offered a kind and genuine smile to Phil. "If you behave yourself and let the doctors and nurses do what they need to, you can have a turkey sandwich and a warm shower after your tests are completed and we're sure that you're okay." Underneath it all, Rachel was very concerned for Phil. He was a 'frequent flyer', seen in the ER several times a week for alcohol intoxication. He panhandled money on street corners and made enough to overdose daily on alcohol. She hoped this time was just another drunken fall. He had fallen so many times over the years, his face was permanently deformed. Numerous attempts of placing him in rehab had failed.

A steady stream of patients walked into the triage area all afternoon. Chest pain, trouble breathing, abdominal pain, coughs, colds, sore throats, STD checks, pregnancy checks, falls, sports injuries and lacerations in need of suturing. It was a typical day in the ER.

It was seven o'clock and time for shift change when a first year college student wandered in. "What brings you to the ER?" Rachel inquired.

The teen answered, "I have started having abdominal cramps and had one episode of diarrhea after eating a 7-11 burrito for lunch about five hours ago."

Within five minutes the young man was back at the triage desk, complaining to Rachel, knowing full well that they were in the middle of shift change. "I just had a little more diarrhea. I don't know why people are being taken back before me, when I came in first?"

Rachel replied calmly but firmly, "We are changing shifts, so please have a seat. We'll check your chart as soon as we finish giving report."

The student retorted, "But I've been here for thirty minutes already. I now have to wait for another shift to start? I'm calling my mom. My dad's a doctor."

Rachel replied, "Then maybe he can tell you to drink fluids and that you'll be fine. Go sit down."

The two nurses continued their change of shift report.

It was finally 7:30, quitting time, when Rachel finished giving report to the oncoming nurse assigned to triage. On her way out, Rachel stopped by room 2 to see how Phil was doing. She looked in and saw a ventilator assisting his breathing through a tube that had been inserted in his airway. Two nurses from the Neurosurgical Intensive Care Unit were preparing to take him to his room, explaining to Samantha: "We're going to the Operating Room to drill burr holes into his skull to relieve pressure on the brain from the blood that is compressing brain tissue. The CT scan showed a subdural hematoma with a midline shift."

Nodding to her from inside the room, Samantha's eyes were full of tears as she placed Phil on a portable cardiac monitor to prepare him for transport to the ICU. The young nurse was clearly overwhelmed that she had let the patient down by prejudging that he was on another drunken bender. Samantha gazed at Rachel with a newfound respect, and Rachel hoped that she had learned not to make assumptions about her patients based on preconceived biases.

On the ride home Rachel's thoughts wandered to David, wishing she could see him that night. Knowing he was on night work, she arranged to have dinner and drinks with Addie at their favorite hangout, The Whistling Oyster. Rachel parked her car in front of their apartment. She ran the short distance to meet Addie, the frigid winter wind slowing her pace as she tucked her head down and tried to run against it. The cold licked at her face and crept under her clothes. Breathless and shivering, Rachel opened the door of the Oyster and rushed in, quickly pulling it closed behind her in an attempt to shut the cold out. She found Addie, giving her a quick hug, and then throwing herself into the adjacent seat while ordering a Knob Creek on the rocks to warm her up.

A few minutes later, David entered the Oyster and joined them. Rachel was delighted, "I thought you were on duty tonight."

David leaned over and kissed her cheek. "Someone wanted to switch so I'm off. I figured you and Addie would be here."

Rachel smiled. "Oh, I bet you can't top this one. You owe me dinner at Tio Pepe if you can't. You'll never guess what happened today."

With a mischievous grin David replied, "I bet someone cut off his penis."

"How did you know?" Rachel disappointedly asked.

David responded: "We received a call to assist the police with a search in an apartment. When I walked into the apartment the female officer said that they were looking for a penis. They went towards the bathroom and the bedroom, and I went to the kitchen. Lucky me, I found it on the kitchen table and called them in. Blood was everywhere; on the floor, on the table, even in the sink with a blood covered knife and a bloody razor blade. The female officer stood and stared at it for a full minute before replying, 'The hospital wants us to bring it in so they can reattach it. My momma told me not to take this job.' Watching her try and decide what to do was painful so I took pity on her, put gloves on and just scooped up the bloody, shriveled piece of skin. I put it in a bag and put the bag on ice. But, you know how firefighters are, you pick up just one penis and you never live it down, I now have a reputation."

Rachel laughed so hard, tears streamed down her cheeks. "Well, your secret is safe with Addie and me; however, I'm sure that by now the entire Fire Department has heard about it."

David replied, "I guess you owe me dinner at Tio Pepe now."

Frank walked in to the Oyster and gave Addie a kiss on her cheek. David and Frank ordered drinks and David repeated the penis story for Frank. "I've seen many unusual things in my years as a firefighter; but, nothing that tops this. You just can't make this kind of stuff up."

The four of them sat and talked until the Oyster closed for the night, then they all walked back to Addie and Rachel's apartment, brewed coffee and made a pizza. As they continued their pleasant conversations, Rachel looked around at the other three people who were sitting in the living room with her thinking, "How did I ever get so lucky to find three such good friends? Well, really two great friends and one wonderful boyfriend? Life is good!"

Chapter Eleven: Girls For Sale

"...It is a capital mistake to theorize before you have all the evidence. It biases the judgment."—Lessons from Sherlock Holmes: Don't Decide Before You Decide

One Saturday night, Addie was at home making dinner when her cell phone rang. She answered, only to hear the familiar background noise of the emergency room of monitors beeping, inaudible multiple conversations, and the overhead speaker of the hospital operator requesting designated staff to assist with a crashing patient in some area of the hospital.

The charge nurse was on the line. "Addie, hey, it's Susan, hey, I've got this fifteen-year-old girl, well at first she said she is thirteen then quickly changed her answer to fifteen years old. Anyway, her name is Shelly Willoughby. She's in room 1 with a gunshot wound in her arm. She has been brought in by her so-called 'boyfriend.' But something doesn't seem right. Not only does the guy answer for her, but he seems too old to be hanging out with a teenage girl. She's dressed much older than I would expect a thirteen or fifteen year old, but these days it's so hard to tell. Maybe he is her boyfriend, I really don't know. When I asked the girl if the police were called, she said nothing but looked at him. Again he answered for her, 'No, you don't need the police. It was an accident. Nobody shot her. Bitch shot herself.'"

"Okay, yeah, I agree Susan," said Addie. "Something doesn't sound right. This is a mandatory report; the police have to be called."

"Addie, remind me again what is mandated to report in Maryland?" Susan asked.

Addie explained, "Any injuries involving boats, bullets, and suspicious burns need to be reported to police. Go ahead and call 911 but don't let on to the patient and the so-called 'boyfriend' know that you're calling. I don't want him to take her and leave. I'll be there in about 40 minutes. If you could get her medically cleared by the emergency pediatrician and make sure they get X-rays of that arm. Please don't clean the gunshot wound and do not let anyone cut through her clothing near the bullet wound either. I'll see you in a few!"

"Okay, thanks, bye." And Susan hung up.

Addie arrived and found the girl and her alleged boyfriend in emergency room 1. The young girl had a youthful face, with big round eyes and dimpled cheeks. The girl must have recently turned age thirteen, Addie thought; no way was she fifteen years old, based on her rounded chin and underdeveloped cheekbones. The tight white mini-dress with a low cut neckline and cleavage pushing out from an overly padded bra was quite inappropriate for the young teen. The girl's hair was long and blond with bleached highlights in the front; it appeared to be straightened by someone who knew how to professionally style hair. As Addie drew closer to the girl she noticed remains of red lipstick staining the young girl's small lips. Addie also discerned eyelash extensions, making the child's green eyes appear larger and more childlike. Tear marks remained in the girls heavy makeup, streams of tears she must have shed after being shot hours earlier. The once innocent girl's nails were nicely done in gel French tips. Addie was confused by the fact that the girl's features were that of a very young teen but her appearance did not match. Addie wondered, "Who is spending so much money on this girl? Someone is taking good care of her. Too good of care."

The girl was sitting quietly on the stretcher; she was unemotional, which Addie found quite strange for a middle school age girl after "accidentally" shooting herself. She was expecting the typical melodramatic, crying, overly sensitive thirteen-year-old girl with a bullet wound in her arm. The "boyfriend" was also quiet. His eyes glared around the room while his head stiffened.

Addie asked him, "What's your name and how are you related to her?"

He abruptly answered in a defensive tone, "Smiley. None of your business." Under his breath, with a sigh he gruffly mumbled, "Bitch." His harshness made Addie uncomfortable. She felt flushed and the hairs on her arms were standing on end by the unpredictability of his behavior. He was dangerous. Addie quickly dismissed the notion that the guy was the young girl's boyfriend. The teen remained melancholic, sitting with her head down, staring at the floor.

Addie decided to ignore him and introduced herself to her young patient. Leaving to get her forensic camera, Addie shared a gentle smile at the scared child, hoping to make her feel more comfortable. The girl was still looking down at the floor when Addie walked by the room on her way to chat with Susan, the charge nurse. Before she could ask Susan if the police had arrived, she saw two uniformed officers coming down the hall.

Addie approached the police. "Hi, I had the ER call you for a report of a gunshot wound. The so-called 'boyfriend' says it's accidental and that she shot herself, but I think there's more going on here. I haven't talked to her yet, she seems scared and he keeps answering all of my questions for her. I need your help in getting him out of the room so that I can talk to her, but we also need to get to the truth about this gunshot wound. I need to know what happened and how far away the gun was when it went off. The guy that brought her here seems quite possessive over her. If you can ask him what happened and how far away was the gun when it went off, I'll ask her the same questions. Afterwards, I can evaluate her gunshot wound to see if their stories are consistent with the characteristics of the wound. The orthopedic surgeon is on his way. He'll probably want to get her to the operating room as soon as possible in order to remove the bullet."

One of the police officers said to Addie, "I'll take him, what's his name? 'Smiley'? I'll take 'Smiley' and put him in the back of my car, run a check for warrants, and see what he tells me about the shooting. I'll call your cell phone once I know more. The other officer will stay in the room with Miss Willoughby. I'm going to call in our corporal. He has experience in human sex trafficking and he'll be a big help to us. I'll run a missing persons check to see if she has been reported missing."

"Okay," Addie responded. "Miss Willoughby will stay in the main emergency room. We will be in room 1 for now. Once we have more information, we can decide what our next move will be, but I'm thinking Homeland Security, the FBI. Of course we will wait until your corporal arrives, and he can advise us further."

Addie entered the room. The young girl was quietly sitting on the stretcher. The police officer was standing guard in the room. A white gauze bandage wrapped around Shelly's right upper arm had a large area of red blood seeping through. Initially, the girl did not make eye contact with Addie. Suspecting that the young girl was being trafficked, Addie spoke calmly. "You're safe here Shelly. We will help you. We want to help you to get away from him. You need to help us by answering my questions. I know you're scared, and you're probably very confused and not sure who you can trust. Do you know where you are? Can you name the county and state?"

The scared child stared at Addie, eyes are welling up with tears. By the petrified look on the girl's face, Addie immediately sensed Shelly has been sold into child sex slavery. Addie put her hand on the scared child's left shoulder and leaned in, reassuring her that she has been saved, "We can help you get away from him, from all of them, you're safe now. Do you know what state you're in?"

Shelly half stuttered. "I saw a sign for Maryland, but I don't know where in Maryland I am."

"How did you get to Maryland?" asked Addie.

"In a van, a white van. We were in the back and covered with a blanket," replied Shelly.

"Who is 'we'?"

Shelly spoke hesitantly. "My friend. I can't talk anymore, they will kill her. Let me go, I don't want to talk to you anymore, everything's fine. I'm okay."

The girl's cell phone rang with "Rilla1" displaying on the screen. The girl visibly panicked. She glanced about, frantically moving her stuff around, trying to gather her belongings to leave; the monitor showed her heart rate shoot up to 160 beats per minute. She was in an instant state of fear. The officer immediately grabbed the phone and turned it off, disengaging the GPS. Addie's intuition that the girl was being trafficked had just about been confirmed. She realized she needed to get the child to safety and away from her pimp who, judging by the name "Rilla1" was a gorilla pimp.

"Get your things, we're moving to another room," she said to the child. Addie's heart was racing, wondering where "Rilla1" was and why was he calling?

Addie slowly opened the door to the exam room, glanced up and down the hallway before leading her young, scared patient to a locked treatment area of the emergency room. They made the short walk across the hallway into the locked pediatrics unit. The girl was now safe and secure. Addie left her with a pediatric emergency room nurse, instructing the nurse to ask the pediatrician to order STAT portable x-rays of the right arm. Addie also instructed the nurse not to clean up the injury, preserving the injury exactly how it looks so Addie could take a few photographs for documentation.

Addie then enjoined the police officer standing guard in the room, "Please do not let anyone move the girl from this room until the suspect is secured." Addie left to look for the police officer who was talking with the suspect.

Addie walked outside of the emergency room where police usually park. She approached the officer to inform him of her concerns. They spoke privately in the parking lot while the suspect was in the back of the patrol car. "Hey, I suspect this girl is being trafficked as a child sex slave. I asked what her mom's phone number is and 'Smiley'..." Addie pointed to the patrol car, "...answered for her. He gave false information, regarding her home address and phone number, to the hospital registration clerk. She doesn't have any identification. She's very thin and looks anorexic. She is withdrawn and seems fearful and anxious, avoiding eye contact with me. She is groomed much more like a 25-year-old, not a fifteen-year-old. I don't believe she's fifteen, I think more like twelve or thirteen based on her youthful facial features. I am interested to see the contents of her purse. These are a lot of signs she has been held against her will and sold into child prostitution. She and a friend were brought to Maryland, concealed by blankets in a back of van."

The officer listened intently, jotting down notes in a small notepad. Addie continued. "I have moved her to a locked area and turned off her phone. A "Rilla1" called her, so the other officer shut her phone off, and she freaked out; she's scared to death."

The officer nodded. "He's handcuffed and in the back of my patrol car for an outstanding felony warrant in Ohio. I suspect sex trafficking, too. The outstanding warrant is for operating a prostitution and drug ring."

"We need to find out where they are staying," said Addie, "because she mentioned a friend was with her and they threatened to kill the friend if she gave us any information."

"I searched him and found a hotel key for a dirtbag motel over near Joppa Road, right off of 695," the officer stated.

Addie thought a moment, then said, "I think I know the hotel. The location is perfect for sex and drug trafficking, right off of interstate 695 and equidistant to Interstate 95 and Route 70. Easy routes from Florida to New York, and out to Ohio. We get quite a few strangulations from domestic disputes from the hotels off of Interstate 695. We have had several sex trafficking cases from there in the past. Big drug and prostitution area. We have to move quickly! I'll go get more information from our girl."

"I spoke with Corporal Greene with the Vice squad and Detective Margo Kim with sex crimes. I filled them in on the situation," the officer informed her. "Corporal Greene will arrange for Vice to head over to the motel by morning. He and Detective Kim should be here any minute now to interview the girl."

All of a sudden Dr. Emory, the orthopedic surgeon, arrived to assess the gunshot wound. Addie entered the room and introduced the young girl to the surgeon. She hoped Dr. Emory did not give her any of his usual passive aggressive crap. Her hopes were instantly shot. Instead of being benevolent, he responded by saying nothing in return to Addie or to the young scared girl. Addie gently asked him, "Please do not clean the gunshot wound until I have a chance to photograph and measure the wound."

He gruffly responded, "What have you been doing? You know she needs to go for surgery?"

Addie took a deep breath. "I know she needs surgery but what do the X-rays show?"

Dr. Emory did not try to hide his annoyance as he mumbled a reply. "X-rays show a low velocity bullet in the upper right arm. She has a nondisplaced proximal humerus fracture with retained bullet fragments. She needs her wound debrided and the fragments removed. At once."

Addie retained her cool demeanor. "I realize she needs to get to surgery, but we needed to secure her and the entire emergency room for everyone's safety, including yours. I suspect this girl is the victim of human sex trafficking. Her best friend, who is barely 13 years old, is locked in a motel by the same traffickers. That child's life is in danger too."

Dr. Emory snapped, "You don't know that! What proof, that she's being trafficked, do you have? None! That doesn't happen here. You're blowing this all out of proportion. I need to get her to surgery."

Addie's voice was firm but implacable. "It will take me five minutes to grab my camera and I'm going to the operating room with her."

"Why, what business do you have in the operating room?" replied Dr. Emory.

"Because this is a criminal case. I need to photo document the bullet being removed and collect the evidence for police. Miss Willoughby will remain in my presence or the police officer's presence until all of the evidence is collected and she is safe."

"For the love of God… Fine! Chop, chop!" exclaimed Dr. Emory as he stormed off. But he stopped and turned for a final sarcastic word. "How about I just drop it in a metal basin and have someone give it to you, to hear it go clang?"

Now furious, Addie retorted, "How about 'No!' How about, you're destroying police evidence in a criminal investigation! I'm going to the OR to ensure chain of custody and to collect the evidence! Give me a few minutes to get my photos! I don't know what part of this you're not understanding! Don't you have a consent form for her to sign, or to make sure the operating room has your instruments? So, why don't you do your job, and I'll do mine?"

Addie fetched her camera out of a black padded camera case. To lighten the weight of the forensic camera, she put the long strap around her neck. Before she took any photographs of the gunshot wound, she shot a photo of the "information sheet":

Victim's name: Shelly Willoughby
CC #: 1718-69-7081
Forensic examiner: Addie Donovan BSN, RN, FNE, SANE
Detective: Corporal Greene (VICE)
Charges: First Degree Assault, possible child sex trafficking

Addie said to her patient, "Shelly, I need you to sign for consent for me to photograph your injury and the bullet removal. I will collect the bullet for forensic evidence. We are going to take you to surgery to remove the bullet very soon. Have you been forced to have sex with anyone in the last week or two?"

Shelly, while signing the consent form, replied, "I haven't had sex with anyone in about a week."

"There seem to be discrepancies in your story," stated Addie. "The guy with you, what's his name? 'Smiley'? He said this was an accident and that you shot yourself? So, I need to swab both of your hands for gunshot residue."

Shelly, pleading to be believed, cried, "I didn't shoot myself! 'Rilla1' shot me. You can swab and collect whatever you need to." After collecting the gunshot residue swabs from Shelly's hands, Addie turned on the ring light that surrounded the camera lens, shining ambient white light on the gunshot injury.

Addie spoke softly to herself while documenting on the body map, noting the physical characteristics of the gunshot wound. "Stippling or powder grain tattooing from unburned gunpowder noted to the right upper arm in a circumferential concentrated area. Punctate tattooing noted to the right front of the white dress." Examining the entrance wound in the girl's upper right arm on the lateral aspect, she noted the abrasion collar from the bullet passing through the skin.

"Is the abrasion collar and the small pinpoint dots from the bullet burning the skin?" Dr. Emory, the now interested orthopedic surgeon, had returned and was looking over her shoulder.

Addie replied, "No, Dr. Emory, the bullet doesn't burn the skin. Victims often describe being shot by a bullet as a searing pain when the bullet penetrates the skin but not from burning. The bullet creates friction when entering through the skin, causing frictional rubbing, appropriately named an abrasion collar. All entrance wounds, no matter the distance of the gun, have abrasion collars. The small, pinpoint lesions are actually minute abrasions in the skin, which is why they are a reddish-brown color, from blood. They cannot be wiped away. Unburned powder grains abrade the skin; they spread out within a circular border because the unburned powder grains exit the barrel of the gun after the bullet is discharged. They heal without leaving scars because the abrasions only affect the superficial layer of the skin."

"So, if you can't wipe them from the skin then why can't we clean up the wound yet?" inquired the surgeon.

Addie replied, "Even though we have an abrasion collar, a bullet on x-ray, punctate tattooing abrasions, I still want to swab the skin for soot and gunshot residue to confirm that the wound…." She pointed to the girl's right arm injury. "…Was produced by a bullet."

Dr. Emory impatiently commented, "Well, this seems like a lot of overkill to me. I usually clean the wound, wash out the tissue, remove and discard the bullet in the sharps container. Done!"

"You're certainly not doing your patients any favor by not properly documenting the characteristics of the bullet wound," asserted Addie.

"I document that there are burns to the skin from bullet entry," snapped Dr. Emory. "I was taught in medical school that the bullet burns the skin when it enters."

Addie, annoyed at the surgeon but remaining polite, replied, "No. Burning of the skin is caused from the flame coming out of the muzzle when the gun is fired. If the muzzle of the gun is pressed into the skin, it is a full contact gunshot wound. The skin tears apart in a triangle pattern when the gases exit the gun, entering into the tissue, rupturing it apart, causing the triangular shape tears. The flame burns the tissue and skin on the inside of the body. It's quite impressive."

Dr. Emory glared at her with raised eyebrows. Addie continued, "So if you have burns to the skin, then the muzzle of the gun was in contact or close, meaning under six inches away from the skin. Soot is created from the flame, and is deposited on the skin but only in contact and close range as well. If you see soot or burning then you know the gun was within six inches from the victim."

"How far away was the shooter when this girl was shot?" asked the doctor.

"Well, I will ask her how far away was the gun, but based on the characteristics that I see, the abrasion collar from bullet entry and stippling or tattooing from unburned gunpowder embedded in her skin, I would say anywhere from twelve to twenty four inches, so one to two feet but no more than three feet away. Based on the circular area of containment of the tattooing, most likely two feet away. The firearms examiner will be able to determine the distance, I can only guess. I can tell you, though, this was not a self-inflicted gunshot wound. Someone shot her."

"You don't know how far away she was from the shooter? This is all of your speculation. Plus, she said it was an accident, so what does it matter?"

Addie regretted engaging in conversation with the surgeon. Unfazed by his aggressive tendencies, she answered, "From examining her wound, if you look closely." Taking a deep breath, hoping not to explode at the surgeon, Addie and Dr. Emory were narrowly focused on the characteristics of the injury.

Showing Dr. Emory the wound, she explained, "Look closely, there is no soot, no searing, the wound defect in her right arm has an abrasion collar, with a small area of tattooing." Holding up a forensic ruler to measure the diameter across the area of tattooing, "The diameter is 4 inches across. I don't need to know how far away the shooter was, I need to know how far away was the gun." Addie began collecting swabs of the right arm to submit to the crime lab to confirm the stippling is in fact gunpowder. Also by trying to move along with the collection of evidence she sought to dissolve the conversation with the surgeon.

Of the young girl, Addie requested, "Could you please take off your dress so I can submit it to the crime lab?" The most helpful surgeon pulled out his trauma shears out of his scrubs in order to cut off the young patient's dress.

Addie, exasperated with Dr. Emory, snapped, "No! You will disrupt the pattern of bullet residue."

Dr. Emory remarked, "There's no residue there, I don't see any."

Addie, her patience lost, wanted her interaction with the surgeon to end. "Yeah, no shit? That's the job of the firearms examiner! They use 'stuff' to identify it. You don't need to know what "stuff" they use, but if you cut through the bullet hole, then you ruin the pattern of the residue, losing the exact distance of the gun to the victim. If she was dying, fine, cut her dress off. But do so with an ounce of consideration of not destroying evidence and cut the clothing on the opposite of the bullet wound."

Addie calmly spoke to the girl, "Shelly, I need to collect your dress. I will submit it to the police."

Shelly's voice was quivering. "Okay, what will I wear home?"

"Don't worry, we have clothing for you. For now, I will help you put on a hospital gown; it opens in the back." Addie smiled at the girl, helping her get undressed, while securing the evidence in paper bags. Addie immediately noticed that written across her left breast was the word "Rilla1" in black permanent ink. She was unsure where to begin asking, "Where? Why? Who wrote that?"

"Time to go to the OR," insisted Dr. Emory. "You can talk to her when she wakes up."

"No!" responded Addie. "Please make sure no one removes the name from her left breast." Addie was fully aware that traffickers used branding to claim their property. The weight and the stress of the case overwhelmed her. The surgeon's boorishness did not help to ease her tension. Feeling sorrow for what the girl had endured, she thought to herself, "I'm glad I'm on-call tonight. We need to make the call to Homeland Security and get this girl home. The police need to find her friend, and fast. What a horrible case, and I haven't even heard the details yet."

In the operating room, the young girl was under anesthesia and Dr. Emory skillfully extended the incision from the entrance bullet wound. He took a hemostat to probe the tract of the bullet.

The police officer interrupted, "Detective Kim is with Corporal Greene. He called, they're walking into the emergency room now, I told him we are in the operating room, so they are going over to the patrol car to talk to our suspect 'Smiley'. Addie, if you could meet them in the emergency room when we're done. I explained the situation and he has already called for the FBI. Agents should be here in two hours. Until then, we're instructed to keep her safe and in a secured area."

Addie spoke to the surgeon, "Could you please be careful not to handle the bullet with metal instruments." She quickly snapped a few photos of the permanent marker tattoo of "Rilla1" scripted across the young girl's budding breast.

Dr. Emory retorted, "What, do you want me to use plastic instruments? Or my fingers, are they soft enough?"

The surgeon palpated the metal bullet fragment with metal hemostat clamps. Spreading the hemostat clamp attempting to grab the bullet, Addie interrupted his train of thought by exclaiming, "Wait, what the hell are you doing? You're not listening. Not with hemostats you're not! You're going to damage the rifling on the bullet!"

Dr. Emory, irritated by Addie's tenacity, uttered, "For the love of God!" He then manually palpated with his finger and extracted the bullet. Addie was standing near with gauze for him to gently put the bullet on. "There! Are you happy?"

"Why, yes I am." Addie had photographed the entire bullet extraction, step by step. Before leaving she asked the OR staff not to touch any other parts of her body besides her upper arm. "I need to ask her further questions and might have to do a rape kit, so please don't disrupt any other areas on her body. I'll see her in the recovery room in an hour or two. Thanks, everyone, for your help."

The operating room nurses were very pleasant. "Thank you for coming in and helping us." Dr. Emory, suturing the bullet entry wound, said nothing to Addie as she left.

Once she had her evidence, she passed by the patrol officer who was standing guard outside of the operating room. Addie said, "In order to secure the girl's clothing and the bullet, I'm going back to my office and will meet you both in the recovery area."

The patrol officer informed her, "Our Corporal is here and wants to talk to you; he's outside in an unmarked car."

"Okay, let me secure the evidence first and then I will find him." Addie hurried to the secured forensic area and placed the freshly obtained bullet in a dryer, in order to dry the blood and tissue fragments remaining on the bullet. She also places the swabs from the palms of the girl's hands in the dryer to dry before they could be packaged.

As Addie wandered outside of the Emergency Room over to the police parking area she spotted a familiar face. She could not contain an excited smile as she approached the Corporal standing outside of his unmarked police car. Addie called to him, "Hi! Oh my God, I can't believe they sent you!" Addie used to know Corporal Greene as Detective Greene, homicide. The couple had a very fond friendship years ago. Never were the two seen without laughter. Addie always thought he was ruggedly attractive, with a shaved head and bright wide smile, and a deep clear, voice and strong broad shoulders. As Addie drew closer, she thought to herself, "He is still devilishly handsome." Addie not only had a fondness for Greene, she also adored his dog, a specially trained police K-9, yellow Labrador retriever, named Maggie.

Maggie was a beautiful dog with creamy-white fur and a long slender face. She had boundless energy and was always ready to go to work. She loved to wake Greene up at 5:30 am for an hour round of playing ball, snow, rain, or shine. Maggie loved "ball" before any police work would be considered. Greene had a soft, gentle side when Maggie was with him. Addie was drawn to his gentleness, something she had not seen in Cain. Unfortunately, she had been too caught up in trying to keep her relationship with Cain sustained and the engagement period happy, that she had been unaware of how much Greene was attracted to her. The two friends had lost touch after Addie left the Emergency Room in the trauma center. Greene was promoted from detective, leaving the homicide unit, to become the Corporal of the Vice Unit. The timing never seemed right between them.

Corporal Greene's face immediately lit up as he walked toward Addie and gave her a hearty hug and a kiss on her cheek. "I haven't seen you since I was in homicide and you were at the trauma center. If I remember correctly, you were engaged to be married?"

Addie smiled. "Well, the marriage fell through before we made it to the altar. Shortly after, I left Trauma One Regional. I was done with the emergency room and have been working in forensics ever since. And you're now Corporal? I had no idea I would be seeing you tonight. After all these years, it's so good to see you. You look good. I often wondered if you were still with homicide. Let's go back to my office and I will fill you in on this case."

Corporal Greene replied earnestly, "It's nice to see you, too. I left Homicide and went to Vice and have been there ever since. And you went into forensics? It's nice to see that you followed your dream."

Greene's partner approached, petite and lovely in a stylish pant suit. Addie greeted her. "You must be Detective Margo Kim! I have heard so many wonderful things about you. My roommate is Rachel and your sergeant, Kate Moran, is a good friends of ours; we live in the same building. It's so nice to finally meet you."

"It's nice to meet you. We tried to meet up with you at Gatchell's but Kate, Bobbi and I got called out on that 'bus-stop' case. I'm going to talk to 'Smiley' a bit more while you interview Miss Willoughby."

As soon as Corporal Greene and Addie reached her office, the recovery room nurse phoned her. "Hi, Ms. Willoughby is out of the OR and waking up in recovery. I think she can talk to you now."

Addie replied, "Thanks, we'll be right over. Is the police officer still with her?"

"Yes, he is," said the nurse.

"Okay, we'll be right there. Thanks for calling." Addie and Corporal Greene walked to the recovery room and saw the officer standing at the threshold of the door. They entered the room to talk to their young patient to see what information the girl would disclose to Addie and Corporal Greene about the trafficking.

Addie sat in a chair near Shelly. "We need to ask you a lot of questions so we can secure the safety of your friend. What's your name and where are you from?"

Shelly replied, "Ohio. Cincinnati, Ohio. My name is Shelly,

Shelly Willoughby."

"What grade are you in?"

"Eighth."

Addie queried, "You mentioned they will kill your friend. What's your girlfriend's name?"

"Emily. We're in the eighth grade together."

"How did you meet that guy you're with, what's his name?"

Shelly answered, "At the mall. Emily and I were walking around the mall when he and this girl, she was about 15 years old, came up to talk to us. I don't know how old he is, but he goes by the name 'Smiley' and those two seem to be working together. The 15-year-old girl, she goes by the name 'Jay-ce'. They showed us a flyer they had for holiday work for teens. I have it in my purse." Reaching into her purse she pulled out a small bundle of paper buried in the bottom of make-up, cash, a small can of hairspray, condoms and business cards. The flyer was printed on hot pink paper with really colorful dollar signs in green with fun lettering. "We thought it would be cool to work over Christmas break at the mall but we thought we had to be older. They said, 'No, we'll hire you.'"

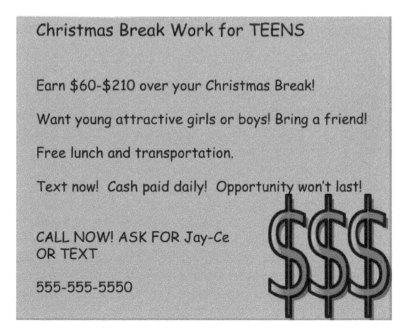

Christmas Break Work for TEENS

Earn $60-$210 over your Christmas Break!

Want young attractive girls or boys! Bring a friend!

Free lunch and transportation.

Text now! Cash paid daily! Opportunity won't last!

CALL NOW! ASK FOR Jay-Ce
OR TEXT

555-555-5550

Shelly went on, "When we were talking to them, I started to get nervous and kept folding the paper up and then I shoved it in my purse. I forgot about it, until now. But they asked for our cell phone numbers and they would call us if their boss said we could have the jobs. Even though 'Smiley' made me nervous, I liked the girl. She was really nice and she was around our age. I trusted her. After an hour she called me, to offer Emily and me the job. She told us to meet her in a hallway in the mall. The hallway was really long and ran behind the food court. The bathrooms were back there. Jay-ce was texting us, telling us where to go. She said the office was back in that hallway. When we opened the door, of what we thought was the office, but it was to the outside and a van was running. Two guys were in the front seats, the side sliding door was open and Jay-ce pushed us in the back of the van. The driver took off as soon as we were in the back but before the sliding door was even closed."

Corporal Greene asked, "This happened in a mall in Columbus, Ohio? You said for 'Christmas break' but it's now March. You've been gone for three months?"

Shelly spoke, sadly, "We were Christmas shopping for my mom, dad and little brother. I haven't seen them since."

Corporal Greene gently smiled, "The FBI has already been contacted. They will help get you reunited with your family. I just need to know, when was the last time you had sexual contact with anyone?"

Shelly looked down. "Two weeks ago."

"Was it consensual or were you forced to have sex?" inquired the corporal.

"I was forced. Every time, I was forced," the child insisted.

"Tell me more about the last time you were forced to have sex," Corporal Greene asked.

Shelly replied slowly, "Jay-ce was in the room with Emily and me. Jay-ce was telling us how she is 'Tone''s wife and we have to listen to her. Then she opened the motel room door and this man was standing there. He was wearing a really nice suit and he had short hair. He gave Jay-ce money. I don't know how much, she counted it and nodded him over to me. I was in a red bra and panties all day. They wouldn't let me get dressed, and now I know why. He came to the hotel room to have sex with me."

Corporal Greene asked, "Is there anything else about the man that you noticed or remember?"

"He smelled of cologne, like he just sprayed it before coming in. It smelled fresh but it hadn't had time to evaporate; it was strong. He could have been one of my father's friends, in his circle. He was wearing a thick, gold wedding ring. He was a little younger than my own father. He was a well-dressed business type of man. His boxer shorts had golf clubs and golf balls on them."

"Did he have a name?" wondered the corporal.

"No, he didn't say much, only what he wanted me to do to him sexually."

"Who is 'Tone'?"

"He's like the main pimp. Everyone follows what he says. He gives the orders. He was calling my phone; he's 'Rilla1'."

Addie asked, "Did he write his name on your chest?" Corporal Greene looked at Addie, eyebrows raised with a question in his face. "She has in permanent marker his name in script across her breast."

Shelly nodded "yes" while sadly looking down at the ground, embarrassed. Exhausted from the lack of sleep and lack of proper nutrition as well as the stress of being shot, Shelly was flat and monotone as she recounted her ordeal.

Greene inquired, "Is 'Tone' or 'Rilla1' the one who shot you in the arm? Tell me everything you remember."

"We were in the motel room last night," said Shelly. "There was a party the night before that continued into the morning. Condoms and condom wrappers were on the floor and empty bottles of beer and vodka. 'Tone' went out to get food. Whatever he gets is what we eat. We don't have a say in anything. All of us girls eat when he decides to feed us. I haven't eaten in two days except for a slice of bread he threw at me yesterday, like a dog. Last night, 'Tone' told us to clean up the room. All of us girls, it was four of us. Me and Emily and two new girls. The two new girls were forced to have sex with guys at the party. We were still wearing slutty clothes from the party. 'Tone' was mad about how trashed to room was, but the men he brought in to have sex with the new girls were the ones who trashed the room. 'Tone' put all of the clothes that we had to wear into a black trash bag. He took the clothes with him so that we couldn't change our clothes. I was sick to my stomach from the bottle of vodka they made me and Emily drink. I came out of the bathroom after throwing up. I heard someone banging on the door, Jay-ce told me to open it. So I opened the door and 'Tone' was standing there with his gun pointed at me. The gun was extra-long with a black handle which he pointed at my face. He was yelling that Jay-ce texted him that me and Emily wouldn't clean up the room. That's not true, I was throwing up. I couldn't clean up anything. Every time I leaned over, I started throwing up again. 'Tone' was yelling at me, telling me that he spends too much money on me and I was a little bitch for not obeying him, then shot me. Shooting me in the arm, and said, 'That's what you get for not listening; next time it's in your head.' Usually he will beat any girl that doesn't listen. He's always punching one of us. He said that he will take my little brother and sell him, just like he does me, if I ever leave. He also threatened to kill Emily if I tried anything today. He beats us, he makes men have sex with us, sometimes I have sex with four to six men a night, sometimes more. Some of the men are business type, really rich and nice suits, and they are allowed, if they pay more, to beat us up. Some men are fat, old or smell bad and really gross. I want to throw up when they put their mouths on me and when they force me to put my mouth on them. 'Tone' and Jay-ce make me and Emily drink shots of vodka before men show up for sex. Jay-ce took me to the mall to try on sheer or lacy bras and panties. Everything matched and was either black or red. I didn't realize it was March already. I'm not even sure where I am, besides in Maryland. I'm sorry, I was telling you that I was trying to clean, but I just couldn't stop throwing up. He told 'Smiley' to take me to the emergency room and say he's my boyfriend."

Greene asked quietly, "Did anyone have sex with you last night?"

Shelly said, "No. Over the last two weeks we went to Ohio and New York where 'Tone' and Jay-ce were getting new girls. All around my age, some younger and some a little older than me."

"Were they prostituting the new girls?" asked the corporal. "Why didn't they didn't sell you in the last two weeks?"

She explained. "They were selling the new girls for sex and had me and Emily there for entertainment. Lap dances and to get the men hard. I don't know exactly where they're getting the new girls but we picked them up in New York and Ohio from other people. I guess they stole them the same way they took me and Emily."

Addie wondered, "How far away was the gun when you were shot?"

"I came out of the bathroom and someone was banging on the motel door. Jay-ce said, 'Get the damn door.' So I opened the door and 'Tone' busted in. He had the gun, pointing it in my face, "You ain't gonna clean the fucking room, bitch? All the shit I buy for you? You're mine and do what the fuck I tell you!" Spit was spraying out of his mouth. He could be really nice. Sometimes I liked him and after a while I didn't mind being there. But then he would get angry. I don't know what made him angry. Us girls did everything he wanted us to do."

Addie asked, "Tell me about when you were looking at the barrel of the gun, when it was pointed to you?"

Shelly looked up to ceiling with her eyes fixed, remembering the events. "It was black. The end of the gun was black. I could no longer see who was holding the gun. I no longer heard 'Tone' yelling. Everything was quiet. I was staring in the end of the gun, the open hole, wondering when a bullet would come out. The gun was about a foot and a half away. The next thing I remember is hearing a loud 'pop' like when you blow up a plastic bag and pop it, it makes a quick, loud noise. Suddenly, I was focused on what was going on in the room. I heard Emily screaming and crying. Jay-ce was screaming, too. That was the first time I saw fear in Jay-ce. I felt burning in my arm, but not too much pain."

Corporal Greene said, "We have notified the FBI and have them coming to pick you up to take you back home to your family in Ohio."

Shelly, with tears flowing in streams down her face, hugged Addie. "Thank you, thank you so much for saving me! I was so scared."

Addie said, "Can I put you in a wheelchair and take you to the forensics department? There is a stretcher you can rest on. I have plenty of snacks for you, too. And we can pick out an outfit for you, too, finally, to go home in."

"Yes, I can get into a wheelchair."

"How's your pain?"

"It's not bad; they just gave me a pain pill."

Addie spent her time typing up her report, including all of the details Shelly told her about the traffickers so it was completed to hand over a copy to the agents. Greene sat in the office with Addie, working on his report on his laptop. Addie commented, "I did not ask too many detailed questions for fear of crossing the line between questioning for medical treatment and questioning for investigation by law enforcement."

Greene nodded. "Thanks, I appreciate it. I still can't believe we got to work together again. I have thought about you now and then. So, fill me in, what are you up to? Are you seeing anyone?"

"I am involved with someone and we're pretty serious." She wished that was the absolute truth. Addie was torn about wanting a serious relationship with Frank. She was unsure how to separate working horrible sex crimes and creating normalcy in her personal life. Sometimes she wished for one moment where the world would seem to stop, so she could feel alive again. "I have often thought about you and have always cherished our friendship. There must be a reason why time keeps skipping us."

Two FBI agents, in plain clothes, entered the forensics unit with security, arriving under the two hour mark. The agents were casual, wearing dress pants and short sleeved polo shirts, unlike typical FBI agents, who wore suits and London Fog rain coats. The agents were nice and Addie could tell they had certainly done this before, finding missing children, and taking them home. Corporal Greene and Addie chatted outside of the room while the FBI interviewed their latest victim of human sex trafficking.

Greene, with excitement in his voice, told Addie, "I just heard from Vice, they got a view of her friend in the motel room. They saw other young girls, too. Vice along with SWAT will be making a move at the break of dawn to rescue them. Hopefully, by the end of the day all of the girls will be home and can sleep in their own beds."

Addie sighed, "I sure hope you're right."

Walking to Greene's unmarked car they chatted, Greene declared, "I'm going to head over to the motel. We'll bring the other girls over today for forensics, once we rescue them. It was really nice to see you. Time certainly stands still when we're together."

Addie chuckled. "When I went outside, I couldn't believe you were standing there! I often wondered if you were still in homicide, and what you were doing. Aside from committing a murder, I wasn't sure how to reach you. You know, the time passes. I am so glad you will be on the squad that is saving the young girls; your gentleness will be comforting to them." Addie gave Greene a gentle but long hug, appreciating what a wonderful detective and friend he was. His was a compassionate soul, especially in regard to the child victims.

Before strolling away, Addie said, "I'm off today, but I will phone the on-call forensic nurse, giving her the information that a raid may occur and I'll get a team together to get the evidence collected on the two other girls. Hopefully, by tonight all four of these children will be home safely. Thanks for doing this job. You really are the best!"

The FBI agents exited the room, updating Addie. "Shelly Willoughby is on the missing and exploited children list. Her family reported her missing the day before Christmas. She is twelve years old. Agents have been sent to Miss Willoughby's home to contact the family, letting them know that we found her, alive and well. You know, your suspicions were right and if you were not on-call tonight, this girl might have been sent back to her traffickers."

Addie nodded, explaining, "My team of forensic nurses is trained in recognizing and handling human trafficking cases."

The FBI agent stated, "Shelly told us that she had been seen in another emergency room and had one other visit to an urgent care center. She wasn't able to tell them she was kidnapped and being forced to prostitute while being held against her will. Not one doctor or nurse recognized the signs of human sex trafficking. Otherwise they would have known to report to child protection services and call the National Human Trafficking Hotline."

The FBI agent pulled a small laminated card from his pocket, handing it to Addie, asking, "Could you please distribute the information to the Emergency Room staff?"

"Yes, what information specifically should I relay? I can make a reference sheet for the ER staff."

The agent told her, "Shelly said she was seen at an urgent care clinic for chlamydia, and the doctor was very judgmental. She told me that the doctor made comments like 'she's lucky all she has is chlamydia if she's having sex for money.' Look here on the information card, and please forward this to the ER staff and pediatricians, according to the National Human Trafficking Hotline.org: 'Sex trafficking is a form of modern day slavery in which individuals perform commercial sex through the use of force, fraud, or coercion. Minors under the age of 18 engaging in commercial sex acts are considered victims regardless of force, fraud, or coercion. Minors under the age of 18 engaging in commercial sex acts are considered victims regardless of force, fraud, or coercion.' She was seen in the emergency room for a broken nose while prostituting. Shelly said that no one during the other two visits made 'Smiley', who is one of the lower pimps, or fraud, or coercion. Minors under the age of 18 engaging in commercial sex acts are considered victims regardless of force, fraud, or coercion.' She was seen in the emergency room for a broken nose while prostituting. Shelly said that no one during the other two visits made 'Smiley', who is one of the lower pimps, or Jay-ce, the 'bottom girl' in the trafficking world, leave the room to talk to Shelly alone. You are the first nurse to separate Shelly to reassure her that she was safe. The first medical person to recognize the signs that she was being trafficked. She might have left here again being discharged 'home' to her traffickers. She owes this all to you and your recognition of what a human trafficking child victim looks like: it looks much like a child prostitute."

NATIONAL HUMAN TRAFFICKING HOTLINE
888-373-7888
POLARIS PROJECT
www.polarisproject.org

Chapter Twelve: The Mediation

"Music is the mediator between the spiritual and the sensual life."
—Ludwig van Beethoven

Addie was enjoying her day off, still in her pajamas and on her second cup of coffee, when her phone rang. Her heart leaped as she heard Frank's voice. "Hey, good morning! I heard from Kate Moran that your case took the plea deal."

"Yes he did. He got fifteen years with eight years suspended. We have been so busy with cases and then the human trafficking/child sex ring came in. I was able to assemble a team of three forensic nurses and one victim advocate in less than thirty minutes! Our team is the best, and incredibly dedicated. The forensic nurses had all four of the sexual assault exams done in about twelve hours. Our unit has been so busy. I forgot all about the trial from, what, three weeks ago?"

"I'm sure your photos and report helped the defense to encourage him to decide to take the plea deal." Frank sighed.

"I'm so glad he didn't prowl The Whistling Oyster. That's where Rachel and the girls and I like to meet up for drinks, if we don't want to make the drive up to Gatchell's. He would have tainted it for us, forever!"

Frank laughed. "Gatchell's is like ten minutes from Fell's Point. You girls can't drive ten minutes?"

Addie replied, laughing "Nope. Ten minutes is a far drive through the city when we can walk to The Whistling Oyster."

"We should grab a drink at the Oyster."

"Yes, we should! Just you and me? How about tonight?"

"Yeah, I'll pick you up at your apartment. What are you, Thames and Wolfe?"

"Yes, come over at 8 pm and we can walk," suggested Addie. "It's a straight walk down Thames Street."

"Babe, I'll see you tonight."

"I'll see you tonight at 8."

Rachel called from her room, "Hey Addie, was that Frank?"

"Yesssssss!" Laughing and yelling happily, "He's coming over tonight! I am so excited!"

Rachel answered, "I'm going out with David tonight. So, do you think Frank is the one?"

"Rachel, I am so in love with him. He's the one for me. I can't imagine anyone else."

Frank arrived at Addie's building promptly at 8 pm and saw her waiting outside of her apartment building on the corner of Thames and Wolfe Street. Addie appeared calm from the outside but inside she was consumed with total excitement and slight nervousness as she watched Frank stride towards her. It was an unusually warm winter evening; the fog was dense from the warm air rolling over the damp streets. The pubs were barely peeking through the white sheer curtain of fog, typical for Fell's Point because of the waterfront being so close to the eighteenth-century cobblestone streets. The street lights were dimmed but yet beyond the veil of fog the sky was illuminated.

Frank paused as if taken aback by Addie's appearance, with her blond hair curving to the contour of her face, resting just below her shoulders. She wore a black leather jacket, zippered half way over a fitted navy blue dress that hugged her slender body, with high heels which accentuated her toned legs. They casually strolled the cobblestone street to The Whistling Oyster and found seats at the bar. Addie gracefully perched on the barstool, turning slightly towards Frank, resting her right arm on the bar after she put down her black leather clutch. He handed her a cocktail menu. After ordering, she placed the menu on the bar and relaxed in her chair, trying to seem more at ease, by folding her hands together and interlacing her fingers. She noticed his eyes run over from her face to her legs, as she sat facing him. It was as if they both realized that their dedication to their work had caused them to deviate attention from each other. But tonight would be different.

Frank put money in the jukebox.

"Pick number 54," Addie called out, with a big grin. Patsy Cline's "Crazy" began to play. Addie laughed with delight at the puzzled expression on Frank's face. He burst into laughter, too. Frank ordered a Manhattan and Addie ordered her usual, a whiskey sour with an extra cherry. They enjoyed each other's company and conversation as they sipped their drinks. Frank reached for Addie's hand, giving it the most subtle, gentle caress.

Lenny Kravitz's "It ain't over til it's over" started to play. Frank stood up, extending his hand to Addie, offering her to dance. She accepted his invitation. Slowly circling the wooden plank floor, concentrating on her rumba box step, the couple made the floor their own. A few locals were at the bar, fondling their drinks, not paying attention to Frank and Addie. One of the patrons seemed happy staring out the picture window at the streetlamps that brightened the cobblestone street under the foggy silvery sky. Another local, while walking by, looked in through the large window, watching Frank and Addie dancing by the vintage mahogany bar, pressed against each other.

Frank had one hand around her waist and his other hand firmly pressing the palm of her hand. Together, with their forearms resting on each other, now swaying side to side, Addie felt her heart beating. Her breaths were deep; her shoulders, straight as she melted into him. "He makes me laugh and fills my soul; I could stay in his arms all night. I love this man," Addie said to herself.

Ending their first drink, Frank said to the bartender, half raising his right hand, "Excuse me, sir, we'll have another." As they sipped their second round of drinks, laughing and talking, a few more reminiscing songs played in the background. Addie wished for the night to never end.

They ambled back to her apartment. Much more at ease leaving the bar than walking to it, Addie held Frank's muscular arm. Due to the exacting nature of their careers, neither could remember the last time they had felt so alive.

"Do you want to come up for a minute?" asked Addie. "The view from the rooftop deck is quite impressive." Frank and Addie entered her apartment, and after she made coffee, they climbed the black wrought iron staircase, passing through to her bedroom to the rooftop deck. The couple admired the view of the Domino's Sugar sign's bright orange lights illuminating and reflecting on the water of the Baltimore inner harbor. The heavy fog seemed less dense on the roof of the four story old cannery building. The round, white full moon was hidden at times behind the dense clouds. When there was a clearing in the clouds, the moonlight was so bright it could cast a shadow. The radiance provided just enough light for Addie to briefly study the contour of his lips and eyes. When peering below at the cobblestone streets, they could see the denseness of the fog, like a Sherlock Holmes mystery in England.

They listened to the sounds of the city, from the faint barking of a dog to a fading police siren, then silence, but only for a brief moment. The stillness was interrupted by the almost romantically deep-patterned bellows from the horn of a distant train, sounding two very long blasts, then a shorter blast concluded by two more very long blasts, echoing over the harbor. Once the train passed its station, all was quiet again. The rumble of car tires, bumping slowly along the cobblestone street below, also vanished in an instant.

"There are rumors that a ghost still resides in the building," said Addie, "a ghost of someone who died in an accident in the cannery many years ago. But I have never seen anything. I hear strange sounds sometimes, like boots walking across hardwood flooring. I think it's pretty neat."

Frank commented, "Apparently, many of the pubs here have their own stories of ghostly residents. My brother saw a woman, well, an apparition of a woman, in one of the local bars. It kinda freaked him out."

"One night a woman was brought in to the ER by medics, she hanged herself in her child's playroom; she was dead on arrival. At that time, I was working the night shift, and I would wear a long flowing yellow isolation gown, to protect my scrubs from splashes of blood, and it provided warmth on cold nights. But for a few months after her passing, in the middle of the night when the ER was quiet and all of the lights were dimmed, I would feel someone brush up against me and I would see movement of the yellow gown. The hair on my neck and arms would stand on end. I could feel the energy from the woman's spirit. The suicide woman's spirit roamed the emergency department, specifically room 10, for a few months. I told her she could move on and then I never felt her spirit again."

"Yeah, I believe in all that stuff, too," said Frank. "From working homicide, some of the deaths are so horrific; you can't imagine spirits moving on so easily. I too have seen some bizarre things. It's cool stuff, that is, if you believe in it. Which I do." He paused. "It's getting late, I should go." He leaned towards Addie.

"I guess so," Addie whispered.

"Yeah," responded Frank, wrapping his arms around her, to give her a hug 'goodbye'. Addie's rational thought was subverted by the intoxicating scent of his skin; she leaned in, unable to refrain, and softly kissed his neck. Time had seemed to stop momentarily, as she absorbed his presence. The city was silenced. A whirlwind of happiness blew by, and at that moment no one else in the world existed. He gently ran his fingertips along the side of her neck, just barely touching her skin. Her left hand caressed his arm, feeling his strength from within, wondering if she will get to see the tattoo on his bicep that she has only seen glimpses of beneath his shirt sleeves. She stopped and gazed up at his deep blue eyes, expressionless. He placed his hands gently on her face as his lips gently brushed hers, still sweet from the whiskey sour, and they became lost in their first passionate kiss.

Chapter Thirteen: I'll Be Watching

"The belief in a supernatural source of evil is not necessary. Men alone are capable of every wickedness."—Joseph Conrad

On some nights, Addie would work in her office until three or four in the morning. She would keep her office door open because their hallway was private, except for security, but the guards hardly came around at night. She functioned better at her office, especially at night when everyone was gone. Well, just about everyone except the night staff. One night, it was almost 2 am. She was finishing a case and heard footsteps and a door slam. She peered out of her office and saw no one. So she opened the door at the end of the hall and peeked out. No one was there except Dr. Emory, walking slowly down the hall, typing something into his phone. She supposed he must have had a late surgery to perform.

Addie returned to her office. She was almost finished typing up a twenty page report about an attack on an elderly woman that was particularly brutal. Her mind was so exhausted and raw from the horror of it that it was by sheer will power alone that she was able to keep typing and recording the facts of the case in meticulous detail. She knew that she would not be able to sleep unless she finished. She sighed and forged on. Nursing was a tough job; she loved her job, but she understood that if she came to work seeking mere human gratification she would have quit long ago. And yet it was a gift. She was grateful for the gift of being able to help someone at the worst time of their life. And even for the little things she was grateful, such as the gift of knowing how to respect the boundaries of a fearful child until gaining their trust.

Addie typed the last sentence and with a few clicks of the mouse began printing a hard copy of the report. While listening to the gentle whir of the copy machine, she thought of how nurses, detectives, and prosecuting attorneys, those who had chosen to work with victims of crimes, had chosen a career that required compassion and empathy. They were called to help someone at the nadir of their life and to be strong for them.

"We are not heroic in what we chose to do," she thought to herself. "It is a thread that runs through all of us who have chosen to care for victims of violent crimes, one which we cannot deny. We cannot turn away from wanting justice and ultimately peace. Those who lack compassion and empathy usually don't enjoy this line of work, it truly is a gift. By trusting us, we dissolve their fear. We are the first step towards helping them gain trust in themselves, trust in humanity and even trust in their faith."

Addie heard footsteps again and glanced up. Jerry the security guard was standing in the doorway of her office. It startled her; she wondered why he had come into the secured forensics area. Towering nearly six feet tall, and overweight, he filled the doorway.

"Did I frighten you?" Jerry asked.

"Oh, hi, Jerry," she answered with a nervous laugh. "I'm surprised to see you, that's all."

He stared at her with fixed concentration. "I am just checking on you; I could see from the camera you were down here working." Addie had never noticed how odd, really odd, Jerry's pale blue-gray eyes were, especially at night. Perhaps it was the lighting or the late hour, but they were almost cloudy, like of the eyes of a corpse. It made her stomach turn to know that he had been sitting in the security office watching her, maybe for hours. But...it was just Jerry. She knew Jerry. She did not understand why she suddenly felt so uncomfortable, the hairs on her neck standing straight, sending one strong chill down her spine. It must be that she was too exhausted and not thinking straight.

"Well, that's kind of you to check on me. I was just wrapping things up here and was about to call it a night."

"Would you like me to walk you to your car?" he asked.

"Oh, thank you but no. I don't mind walking out alone. But, thanks, anyway."

"Your safety is my duty, Addie," Jerry said in a strangely quavering tone.

Addie locked the kit in the evidence locker. Placing the report in her work bag to drop off to Frank, she confidently strode towards the door, hoping Jerry would stand aside. He did. "Goodnight, Jerry," she said, heading towards the exit.

"Goodnight!" he replied in a subtly aggressive tone, causing goose bumps on her skin.

Addie walked steadily, not wanting to look like she was hurrying or afraid. She tried to process her situation. Should she call for help? But Jerry had not done anything. Besides, he was security. He was the one who would respond first to a call for help. Anyway, nothing had happened. She would talk about her odd feeling about Jerry with Frank in the morning. In the meantime, she had to get out of the hospital and into her car. The door was in sight. She reached into her handbag for her car keys. But they were gone.

"Dammit!" Addie swore out loud. She searched her handbag, trying not to panic. No keys. She must have left them on her desk. She had to go back. She reluctantly made her way through the twisting maze of desolate corridors to her office. Jerry was nowhere to be seen. But the keys were not on her desk. She opened every drawer, looked under papers and chairs, and checked the trash can. The keys were gone. It required every last ounce of self-control to keep her from screaming.

Then Addie recalled that she kept a spare car key in a special pouch deep inside her work bag with her files. She had never used it before; it was supposed to be for valet parking or something. She quickly found it and once again began the trek through the hospital to the door. No one was in sight except the charge nurse at the desk, to whom she waved as she passed. The fresh air outside the door was bracing and helped her to relax. There was a faint light in the sky, heralding the coming of dawn. She ran to her car, jumped in, locked the doors and breathed a big sigh of relief.

"See, nothing happened," she said to herself as she started the engine. The radio started playing. "Oh, one of my favorites, Haley Reinhart," she said out loud, while singing…laughing…thinking of kissing Frank on the roof top deck. *"Only fools rush in…I can't help falling in love with you…shall I stay….would it be a sin?"*

"Hello, Addie." She heard a voice both quiet and menacing. Dread ran through her as she glanced in the rear view mirror to see gray eyes transfixed upon her. The once familiar blue-gray eyes no longer had any visible shade of blue, but were pure gray. He reached from behind her seat, covering her mouth and nose with his large left hand. His right hand wrapped around her neck. His great strength made it easy to squeeze her throat, blocking the flow of blood and oxygen. She tried to pull away but could not move.

"You gotta know better than to walk out alone, you stupid bitch!" It was Jerry's voice and Jerry's eyes. He must have stolen her keys and been waiting for her in her car. She tried not to panic. Think, Addie, think! He was too strong for her to fight. She had a Glock 9mm pistol under her front seat. Frantically trying to grab it with her left hand, she felt under the front seat, feeling the metal bar under the seat, then touching the handle of the gun, thinking she would not hesitate to shoot the bastard between the eyes. But she could not quite grasp it. She could not scream, nor talk her way out of it. Not with his hand covering her mouth and nose. She was gradually suffocating. She tried to hyperventilate for even the smallest bit of air, but he was preventing even the slightest gasp. Her vision was tunneling and blurred, and his ugly voice was getting faint. With her right hand, she slammed on the horn with all her might.

"Stop it, bitch!" Was the last thing she heard him say to her as his hand tightened on her neck. He was so strong that with one hand he was squeezing the life out of her. Had she heard Frank's voice? Losing consciousness, she thought she heard Frank. Unable to call out...unable to breath. Unable to gasp for one final breath she lost consciousness, letting go of the pistol, still under the seat, and releasing the horn, everything was silent.

Cold air was filling the inside or her car, the windshield spider webbed with a bullet hole in the center. Addie regained consciousness, blinking a few blinks she realized she was surrounded by blue and red flashing lights and sounds of police radio chatter. The suspect released his grip moments after a bullet had penetrated through the front windshield into his right shoulder, compliments of Frank.

She tried to speak; her voice was hoarse and strained. "It's okay. Don't try to talk," said Frank. "You were strangled. That security guard that everyone liked so much, Jerry, he was waiting in the backseat of your car. Your keys were found on the backseat. He's with medics and will be transported to the ER, then to jail. Don't worry, he's handcuffed and in custody, and crying like a little girl from the bullet in his shoulder!"

"What happened?" she asked, in a strained voice, as medics were helping her onto the nearby stretcher.

"Well, Dr. Emory happened to be at his office window which overlooks the parking lot. It was dark but he could still see enough of what was going on. He saw Jerry Dederico unlock your car and get into it the back seat. He called the police, considering it a break-in. He had been suspicious that Jerry might have been the one who called in the bomb threat. Anyway, I heard the call come out, knowing you were working late, and then I heard the description of your car come out, I raced over. As I pulled up I saw you struggling with Jerry. He was strangling you. I shouted at him to let you go. He wouldn't so I fired through the glass. Injured in the shoulder, he let you go. We rushed in, pulled you out first, then dragged him out."

"Oh, thank God," murmured Addie. "Wait! It was Jerry, our security guard, who called in the bomb threat and then tried to kill me? Who is he, I mean, really? You think you know someone...."

"I want you to get seen in the ER. The medics are ready to go, and as soon as I find out who "Jerry" really is, you'll be the first to know."

"Will you please call my parents and Rachel?"

"Yes." Frank smiled. "I'll let them know."

Rachel rushed in on her day off to do Addie's strangulation exam. Both girls were so happy to see Addie's parents, Sally and Jim. Rachel gave them a welcoming hug as they entered the emergency room. Jim leaned over Addie and said in a calm voice, "Since all we knew was that you were strangled and someone was shot, we called Fr. Fergus and he is on his way."

"Oh, Dad, I'm fine. All of this is not necessary. But thank you." Addie found comfort in knowing she had such wonderful parents, plus blessings from Father Ferg once he arrived.

Addie and Rachel were happy to finally arrive at home that night after hours in the ER.

Addie gasped. "I forgot to give Frank the report from last night's case. It's still in my work bag." She pulled out the 20-page report, body maps included and all. "I'll stop by headquarters and give it to him tomorrow."

Rachel kindly scolded Addie, saying, "You need to get some rest. I'll take your report to Frank. Laura said for you to take this week off. That means turning off your phone, too!"

Addie sighed and slightly shook her head.

The following week, when discussing Dederico in Frank's office, Addie could not help but feel heaviness setting in from her job.

"When we brought Dederico in for questioning, he had the nerve to ask me to call him 'Jerry'," Frank told her.

"How did you know that Jerry called in the bomb threat?"

"We found surveillance video of Jerry in the ER at the time the threat was called in. He was behind a large cart with supplies, watching Vicki's reaction and everyone else's, too. He tried to inquire about the prior seven patients seen for sexual assault, but you ladies are stellar about *not* letting anyone in during your interviews and exams so he had to find another means to victimize. So, he called in the bomb threat. We think it was a ruse to get Beth alone in the ER so he could sexually assault or even strangle her. His crimes were escalating and I feel he was upping the ante to murder. He tried to kill you, Addie! We found on his phone hours of videos of you and your fellow forensic nurses in your office area, sometimes with patients, other times videos of you working. He had been stalking your department for over one year. He will be put away forever, never to see the light of day. But that's not the worst of it...." He paused. "Well, it turns out that he is the creep who ran the Blair Boulevard corridor preying on girls who became vulnerable after leaving the bars. Plus he has a criminal record going back years! He was a deputy sheriff in Colorado but was fired for the sexual assault of a coworker."

"How did he end up working in our emergency room?"

"He lied about his record. He had fake references, a fake driver's license, changed his name, and traveled under different aliases across the country."

Addie paused for a moment. "I can hardly believe it. There he was near our vulnerable patients. I'll never get it out of my mind, Frank. Victims of horrible crimes would come into the emergency room, those traumatized woman, children and men would come here for help after being sexually assaulted. He must have felt it was all pomp and circumstance. Nothing but a parade for him to stand on the side of a street watching people march by with balloons and banners while he patiently waited for a big float of Snoopy to go sailing by. But instead, it was not a parade at all! It was uniformed police officers, forensic nurses, detectives, walking the patient through the ER for medical treatment in order to obtain a forensic history and a very invasive sexual assault evidence collection. He's just one more downcast of our society, one more wicked person."

As months past, Addie and Frank continue working sexual assaults and strangulation cases, the caseload never ending. Some days three cases at a time would show up in the emergency room, some with police, some without, needing forensics and police investigations. Enjoying her relationship with Frank, Jeremy Dederico was far from her mind.

It was her day off, and she was hoping to spend it with Frank. She was drinking coffee and flipping through catalogs, wishing for a new dining room rug for the loft apartment. The phone rang. It was Frank. He said, "Hey, did you see the article in today's paper on Jeremy Dederico?"

"No," said Addie. "You should know by now that I don't watch the news or read the paper."

Frank chuckled. "Then how do you know what's going on in the world?"

"People like you call me to tell me the important stuff. My mother is always asking me, 'Oh did you see the news?' but she's met with silence on the other line, because my answer is always the same, 'No, I do not watch the news or read the paper. Then her reply is, 'and that's why you get stuck in spring snow storms, you at least should watch the weather.'"

"You're too funny," Frank teased. "But you will want to read about Dederico."

"I don't know that I do," responded Addie. "Ever since the 'Jerry' incident, when I'm in the office at night I make sure the door to the forensics department is locked. But it didn't matter, because he had card-access to our department. I can't relive this again. I know we don't have any more Dederico's working as security, but I'm not taking my chances. I'm a lot more careful now. Oh, okay, I'm reading the article now...." And she read aloud from *The Daily Morning News*:

Serial rapist Jeremy Dederico traveled across the country from California to Maryland leaving a trail of crime behind him. Before he was a career criminal, he was a deputy sheriff in Denver, Colorado. He settled on the east coast in the little town of Blair Heights, Maryland, where his crimes of burglary and rape continued. Once in Blair Heights, he found work as a security guard "protecting and serving his community". He took up residence in a gated community.

Addie paused and said to Frank: "There he was, living among his neighbors, who felt protected living behind the gates. All false senses of security." She continued.

On his days off from his work as a security guard, he would prowl and stalk along The Heights on Blair Boulevard. One particular night, a group of girls were celebrating in a bar on The Heights. Staying in a hotel close to the bar, the girls walked back together, thinking 'safety in numbers.' The girls arrived safely to their room, which was located on the first floor and went off to bed. What the girls were not aware of was the man who was watching them while they were in the bar; following them back to their hotel, hiding outside, waiting for them to fall asleep. He was the same man who had been a deputy sheriff. The same man who is now a serial rapist.

Feeling secure that the girls were sleeping, he broke into the room. He entered through the patio sliding glass door. He came prepared, bringing a bag of items to aid him in carrying out the sexual assaults. He had sexually assaulted two of the girls before a third girl woke up and saw him. He fled the scene. 911 was called and the first officer arrived. Dederico was eventually arrested after attacking a nurse leaving the Kings Valley Medical Center during the early morning hours on November 2, 2018.

"Frank, I remember the hotel case. It was one of my first cases, do you remember?"

Frank answered, "Yeah, I remember. I responded to the scene shortly after patrol arrived. The victims were transported to the Kings Valley Emergency Room. I told the triage nurse to call you. That was the first time I met you. All of the girls were traumatized and had difficulty making sense of the horrible acts that took place after a seemingly innocent night out. There were other similar cases across Maryland, DC and Virginia, too. All in high end hotels."

Addie said, "I was glad the two victims came forward to report and had forensic evidence collected. But as a forensic nurse, they were my patients and not just victims. Both of the girls provided a full forensic history and cooperated with evidence collection. The investigation moved so quickly, with the crime scenes of the hotel room and the girls secured, no evidence was lost. I moved at a pace that was comfortable for them during the forensic examinations, and so both girls did great. The girls were traumatized, never imagining they would be raped while safely sleeping in a hotel. I talked to them during the exam, reassuring them that this was not their fault. I really don't think there was anything they could have done to avoid succumbing to being one of his victims."

Frank sighed. "Yeah, he was initially into burglary and robbing people to support his drug habit. But at some point, Jerry decided to up his crimes to include rape. We found DNA at the scene, and you got DNA from the genital swabs of both girls. But since Jerry had never been arrested he wasn't in CODIS. Once we caught Jerry attacking you, we were able to get his DNA and put it into CODIS. He popped up, my God, he left a trail of crime in every state from here to the West coast! But he was going by another name; actually he had a list of aliases he was running off of. When we searched his apartment, we found personal items from all of his victims. His 'trophies of violence'. He started with burglary, needing money for a prescription drug habit, but escalated to burglary with sexual assault. It was a good day arresting him and getting him off the streets. He defines 'serial rapist'. I'm glad he pled guilty to The Heights hotel crime. The judge sentenced him to 50 years in prison. Hopefully, he won't be released, ever! You will need to testify against him and hopefully he'll get an added 10 years or so for what he did to you. We can tack on the bomb threat. Yeah, he isn't going anywhere."

"Another job well done, you do nice police work! And thanks for shooting him and not me!" exclaimed Addie. "But enough about him. My parents would like us both to join them for lunch at their house next Saturday afternoon. You free?"

"I am," Frank replied.

Chapter Fourteen: Longing

"It is a little dark still, but there are warnings of the day and somewhere out of the darkness a bird is singing to the Dawn." — *Paul Laurence Dunbar*

On a glorious warm Sunday morning in early spring, birds rhapsodized while the plants erupted through the ground with their delicate petals already in bloom. As Addie left the hospital, she was weighted with dark memories, in stark contradiction to the newness of the day and the season. Her mind wandered from case to case, recalling the souls she had come in contact with during her career as a nurse. Like snapshots of photos, Addie remembered the hundreds of patients, never forgetting anyone she had ever taken care of. At the forefront of her mind was Shelly and the hell she endured from being a victim of sex trafficking. Then, she recalled one of her first trauma patients, with his forehead ripped off when he was struck by the blade of a hay baler, whose life she was able to save.

Addie remembered washing the feet of a homeless man because they were dirty and sore. She and all of the ER staff were quite familiar with that particular patient. He had a history of multiple drug overdoses and warrants out for his arrest; he often arrived with police. Even so, with his long-standing criminal history, that night he only wanted his feet washed. He didn't want narcan; he had no demand for opiates; he did not need clearance for jail. He just wanted his feet to be washed. The man was sooty gray from his head to his feet from layers of dirt embedded in his skin and clothes. The wretched, bitter, foul stench of body odor and stale urine wafted through the doorway. Addie could smell him before she could see him. She let the man rest on the stretcher while she washed his feet. It was about 4 am; both Addie and the homeless man were very tired. Addie's thoughts began to drift from the calming warmth of the hot soapy water as it floated over her gloved hands. She submerged a white washcloth into a plastic pink basin in order to wash his encrusted, rotten feet. The soap smelled so fresh, the hot water soothing...her thoughts calmly drifted...as she recalled that it is not a nurse's place to judge others. The humbling moment etched itself on her memory forever.

Then she recalled doing cardiac compressions on a man who was burned and charred after accidentally falling asleep when his bed caught fire from his lit cigarette. Addie was unsure why paramedics brought him in, instead of calling the medical examiner's office, for his body was charred black. Addie then was forced to start cardiac compressions and breathing until she could get the ER attending physician to pronounce the man deader than dead. Upon her first chest compressions she had to place her gloved hands over red, bloody melted tissue. His skin was melted away in third and fourth degree burns from the heat of the fire. Black sooty smoke from the burning of the mattress, and from the walls of the man's bedroom, were expelled from his lungs into Addie's face. Homicide Detective Greene arrived just in time to hear the man's ribs breaking from the force of Addie's compressions, cracking the ribs like brittle chicken bones. His life could not be saved. The manner of death was ruled accidental. The cause of death was asphyxiation. The mechanism of death was smoke inhalation.

There was the time when a mother in her thirties, naturally beautiful even in death, committed suicide by hanging herself in her children's play room because her boyfriend broke up with her. Focusing more on the boyfriend than her lovely, sweet child, the distressed mother climbed up onto her daughter's play kitchen and suspended a rope from a pipe up above in the exposed basement ceiling. After tying the rope around her neck, she fell from the child's play kitchen, strangling herself. Her daughter wandered into the basement playroom and found her mother, blue in the face with the rope around her neck. The child called a neighbor, who called 911. Paramedics started cardiopulmonary resuscitation at the scene. CPR was continued by Addie and other ER staff after arrival in the emergency department and placed in room 10. No one wanted to give up, but after about twenty minutes, her death time was called. While looking over the woman's dead body laying stiff and pale on the stretcher, Addie yelled at her silently in her mind, "How could you be so thoughtless and self-absorbed? How could you do this, leaving behind your precious child?"

The deceased woman's ten-year-old daughter, wearing her pink Minnie Mouse PJs, wide-eyed and full of confusion sat at the side of the stretcher, and patiently asked Addie in a soft innocent child's voice, "When is my mother going to wake up?" Addie could not break the devastating news to the child. Addie, along with a police officer and homicide detective, waited for the aunt and grandmother to arrive in order to console the child, before breaking the tragic news. The manner of death was ruled a suicide. The cause of death was asphyxiation. The method of death was ligature strangulation.

Addie continued her sad thoughts, remembering the horrible rape and kidnapping of a young woman one winter's night, the night before Christmas. The first sign of a struggle were the Christmas presents and homemade sugar cookies, cut out shapes of snowmen and angels, cluttering empty parking spaces near where the woman's car was once parked. A bullet, unfired and still in its casing among the cookies, was the detectives first clue the vicious assault occurred at gunpoint. The young woman was putting her Christmas presents and decorated boxes of homemade cookies from her coworkers in the backseat of her car, when a masked man, dressed in black, rushed out from behind a brown lattice barrier. The lattice separated the parking lot from the meticulously landscaped gardens at an upscale country club in a part of Maryland where crime seemingly never happens. The masked suspect accidentally dropped the bullet out of his backpack when he rushed her in a blitz attack, forcefully striking her in the front of her head with the butt of the gun. Blood immediately began flowing down from her caramel colored hair leaving her forehead and nose bright with a bloody stream. She tried running for her life. She tried to run back to the club entrance.

Running after her, he caught up to his victim at the edge of a meticulously groomed garden that he himself planted and adorned with small winter evergreens. He had draped them in white twinkle lights. The lights automatically came on at four thirty, just before dark. The outdoor twinkle lights gave him enough light to rape, beat, blindfold and bind her hands together in the front. After blindfolding her, the assailant dragged her exposed, naked body across gravel and asphalt back to her car, forcing her inside. The terrorized woman was too scared to scream. The country club was closed, for she was the last the leave, so no one would hear her even if she was able to scream. The masked suspect worked as the master landscaper at the country club. He was all too familiar with the grounds. He also knew the time the country club closed and he knew the last employee was always female and always walked out alone. In the dead of winter, the sky was dark by five o'clock. Unsure who the last one to leave that night, he did not care, he just wanted to victimize someone, anyone. He forced her at gunpoint to cram in the passenger floor space of her car. The suspect then drove the woman miles away to a rural area and pushed her naked, bound, blindfolded body out onto the desolate two lane road. A passerby nearly ran over her naked body. Thinking there was a dead deer in the road, the driver slowed and swerved around the bloodied body. Only to realize... a bound, naked woman was lying in the road, alive! The suspect was apprehended by brilliant detectives through hard work and many continuous hours of investigation.

A jury trial started with testimony from the courageous victim and the first responding police officers. Continuing with day two of the trial was testimony by Addie, as the sexual assault forensic expert. The trial concluded with testimony from the detectives who solved the case. What was a surprise to everyone was to see the suspect in person; he was a short, thin little man with an unsuspecting average look. When Addie was sitting in the witness box giving her testimony, directly across from the defense table, she could almost feel the evil radiating from the suspect. The small, but menacing man sat in a large wooden armchair, his head tilted downward with his eyes raised, much like Stephen King's "It". With his pupils shaded by his upper eyelids, he stared directly at Addie during her testimony as she presented the forensic evidence. The air in the courtroom, as if emanating from the deviant predator, was heavy and suffocating. The defense team was strategically located in front of the witness box, upholding the suspect's sixth amendment right, that the accused shall face their accuser.

When asked to present photos to the jury, Addie left the oaken wood witness box, and walked across the courtroom to stand in front of the twelve members seated before her. Big screen televisions were strategically placed throughout the courtroom, displaying a photo album of horror to the judge, jury, prosecution, defense, and spectators sitting in the courtroom. Nearly twenty-five photos of the young woman's bodily injuries caused by the tremendous force used by the suspect, creating large jagged blood drenched rips to the skin in her head and legs, leaving long trails of blood down her face and legs. Abrasions caused by the shearing of her skin from her neck to her hips from her naked body being dragged across a gravel lot. It was as if she were taken through a portal, straight to the depths of Hell, then returned by the same portal, back to her life. How does one ever really recover?

Beginning the forensic explanation of each photo to the jury, the suspect looked over during the initial few photos, but soon he could not look anymore. His small stature appeared to shrink even further, like a scolded child, with his expressionless face looking at the courtroom floor.

After one week of witness testimony, the suspect was found guilty of first degree rape, two counts of first degree sexual offense, kidnapping, and robbery through the use of a handgun and was sentenced to three life sentences. He had a long criminal record and had been given many chances for social reform. Recently released from prison for "good behavior" from a prior violent sexual assault, three life sentences now seemed to be appropriate. The victim was able to now face him, delivering her "victim impact statement."

Victim Impact Statement
From the moment you stepped into my life, with a mask covering your face and your gun pointed at mine, you changed my life forever. There hasn't been a day that goes by that I don't think about you and the caustic deeds you committed against me. I allow my mind to continue your torture and torment of me. I have begun to wither after being in your dark and terrifying presence for just a few hours, when you took it upon yourself to humiliate, dehumanize, and inflict unspeakable pain upon me. Diabolical threads run

deep through you, and like a virus, have tried to attach to me. I carry overwhelming sadness every single day. I have lost many friends, for I am sullen and withdrawn. I am uncomfortable being 'me'. The scars you left on my body, serve as a memento of your infernal unhappiness imposed on me.

One day I overheard two women talking about the body and the soul. I am not religious, but I couldn't forget the woman's conversation and eventually realized, maybe they were right. Maybe my body and my soul are two forms of me. Maybe I can choose whom my soul attaches to. I felt with time, my soul was attaching to you more and more. I was obsessed over what you had done to me. You were in the process of destroying me. I was allowing you to destroy me. I was allowing you to take over my soul. I was no longer 'me'.

I forgive you. These words are very hard to say but I have chosen to forgive you. I will never excuse your demonical actions. But I need to be free from you. I now pray for you. I pray that whatever entity has attached itself to you will one day release its grip from you, so you can be free too. But, I will no longer allow YOU to have a hold on me. I am releasing your grip over me. You are not allowed in my life anymore. You are not allowed in my thoughts. You are weak...get out.

Now, I am free. I will continue to pray that my soul finds what it is missing, But I am free and able to live my life again. The air I breathe is light and refreshing. My throat is no longer tight from your grip. My anxieties have lifted. When I look in the mirror and see the scars that YOU created, I now think... 'you can violate my body but you will never touch my soul.'

Addie remembered the elderly victim of domestic violence who refused to leave his abusive son because he did not want to leave his cats. Addie and Rachel were the forensic nurses called in, by homicide detectives, to render treatment for his injuries and to collect forensic evidence. The abused elderly man was found naked and beaten, left for dead deep in the woods, miles away from his home. Police were called by a concerned neighbor because of the sounds of shrill cries coming from deep within the woods. After the first patrol unit arrived, the officer was suspicious of the son, feeling he knew more about his father's whereabouts then he let on. Making suggestive comments that his father may be dead in the woods, homicide was called in to recover the body. Homicide called Addie after the man was found, by bloodhound search dogs as well as by all-terrain vehicles (ATV's), deep in thickets in the woods. He was found naked and hours from death. Miraculously, however, he was still alive. Addie quickly called in Rachel for backup, knowing this would be a very involved forensic case; eighty-five percent of the elderly man's body was bruised, all in different stages of healing from bright red to purple, to blue to older bruises noted in yellow and brown discoloration. Dirt and debris was scattered all over the man's naked body. Dirt was covering the soles of his feet. The elderly man ran through woods in his bare feet, naked, while running for his life. He had been beaten mercilessly over time.

One of the first questions the man asked Addie and Rachel was if his cats were okay. Once the man realized his cats were safely living with other relatives, he disclosed about the years of elder abuse and violence. His son had been physically abusing him, stealing his finances, and also had an arsenal of weapons at the home. Police were sent to the home to permanently secure the weapons. The son had frequently threatened to shoot and kill his father.

The elderly man went on to live under an alias in an undisclosed location, and was able to see his two cats whenever he wanted. He healed from all of his physical injuries, with no memory of the vicious assault. Due to the lack of physical evidence no one was charged in the crime, even though there was circumstantial evidence.

As Addie's mind recalled all the souls that had touched hers, a veil of sadness and grief consumed her. The heaviness from case after case, weighed upon Addie. The thirst for justice was undying. The horror her patients had endured now kidnapped and abused her, by occupying her thoughts. She decided to attend Sunday Mass in order to cleanse her consciousness.

Walking to the Cathedral, Addie was in awe watching a murder of crows circling around and filling the trees. She walked further and noticed a crow on the ground. The glossy black crow was lying dead in the grass. "Hmm, I never realized how big crows really are, sitting at the top of trees they don't seem so large. And such beauty." It broke her heart to see the crow lying dead; she realized that the crows in the trees were mourning, for in their own way they experienced grief. Unbeknownst to her, she had been walking through a crow funeral. She went on toward the Cathedral.

Addie entered the resplendent Cathedral, lined in pale gray marble walls and shiny gray marble floors; the air light and crisp with the faint odor of incense from the previous mass. Addie inhaled deeply, welcoming the fragrant, luminous air, free from the evils of the world. It was like a moment of frozen eternity, walking down the center aisle to reach the front of the vast cathedral. Addie chose a seat in a pew mid-way down. The building was crowded but since the cathedral was so spacious, people were spread out from one another. Addie needed to be alone; she chose to sit quietly and listen. She assisted at the Mass, sitting, standing, and kneeling. But when she was kneeling, waiting to walk up to communion, she found herself staring at a massive golden crucifix, suspended over the altar, and emotion flooded her being. The choir, echoing throughout the vaulted ceiling of the cathedral, began to sing *of justice...of mercy ...there is a longing in our hearts for love.*

Addie processed up the aisle with her hands together at her chest to receive communion, joining everyone else, who were moving so gradually the line appeared to be swaying. In the communion line, she stared at the immense golden crucifix hanging over the high altar. Captivated by the magnificent cross, she softly sang...*there is a longing for you to reveal yourself to us...for wisdom, courage, for comfort. In weakness in fear be near...*Feeling a warm fullness in her chest, she feared she might burst into tears before reaching the altar for communion. As she received communion, standing in front of the altar, she caught a glimpse of the magnificent crucifix closer than ever. She could see, amid the glory of the ornate detail of the crucifix, Jesus' face and His expression of sorrow. His emaciated, exposed body, hanging by only his hands and feet, nailed to the cross.

Walking back to the pew, she continued singing softly while staring at the pale grey marble floor. Mesmerized by the ecstatic chanting of the choir, she asked God for courage, strength, and for her prayers to be heard. For she was praying for her patients, that they may find peace from the evils committed against them.

After the final blessing, Addie decided to light a candle for all of the lives that had touched hers. Big tears streamed down her face, so many tears she feared they might have no end. Overwhelmed with tortuous emotions of fear, humiliation, sorrow and grief, it was as if she had absorbed the emotions of every patient she had ever cared for. Then the grief of losing Cain suddenly surfaced. Her feelings seemed to come out of nowhere, for she had been able to put Cain out of her mind for over two years.

She struck a match with her trembling hands to light a white offertory candle as the choir sang louder and more angelic than ever before. While watching the flickering flame, Addie breathed and the veil of heaviness lifted. She was no longer a victim of her own sorrow. She offered up everyone who had touched her soul during her life. She especially offered up all of the members of her team, the nurses, detectives, and attorneys. Words crossed Addie's mind, as if she is being spoken to directly: "Don't let your burdens be your inequalities, let them be your strength." Addie took a deep breath before facing the world of crime and sorrow again. A job she could not imagine ever leaving.

That evening Frank and Addie drove the rural country roads, meeting Rachel and David at a local winery for dinner. The couple, knowing they had two hours left of being "on call," decided to take the chance of having a 'crime free' evening. Addie spread a blanket on the grass in front of a five ensemble jazz band that was delightfully playing their saxophone, trumpet, clarinet, and trombone. The sun sank in the horizon. The stars fixed in the sky. String lights danced from tree to tree illuminating the lawn. Fireflies lit up the darkened woods at the edge of the winery. The romantic rhythmic chirping of crickets; some fast and deep while others, the younger crickets, high-pitched and loud.

Rachel brought over a bottle of wine, freshly uncorked, with four wine glasses. Addie finished unpacking a picnic basket full of figs, cheeses, crackers and chocolate, knowing how much Rachel loved chocolate.

Rachel asked, "Addie, are you ready for a glass of chilled Chardonnay?"

"Not yet," Addie replied. "Frank and I have one more hour of call left. As you know, a lot can happen in an hour. Fingers crossed!" Frank took Addie by the hand. As he helped her stand up, the jazz band started playing "What a Wonderful World" as requested by Frank, to Addie's total surprise. He clasped her waist as they both looked at each other and laughed. Addie, not desiring anyone else in the world, enjoyed dancing slowly to the sultry sound of the jazz band. She settled into Frank, wanting the dance to never end.

Suddenly, Addie was jolted from the moment by the all too familiar ring tone, signaling a call from the Emergency Room.

Addie, in a startle, jumped slightly then hurriedly answered her phone, "Hello, this is Addie."

At the same time Frank's phone rang; a police officer was on the other line, briefing Frank on the child he just brought in to the emergency room with paramedics, needing a rape kit and strangulation forensics exam.

The charge nurse of the Emergency Room was on the other end of Addie's phone. "Hi, Addie, I'm sorry to bother you, but police officers and medics just arrived with an eight-year-old female. She was sexually assaulted and strangled, she has small dots, well, petechiae, from her jaw bone up to her eyes. She seems to be in and out of consciousness; it's a miracle the child is even alive."

Addie said, "I'm on my way. I'll be there in about 35 minutes. Do all that you need to do to keep her alive, just please secure her clothing and no procedures below the waist, unless it's to save her life. Please."

The charge nurse replied, "Okay, thanks, the police officer just told me that the detective is on his way too."

Frank and Addie glanced at each other, knowing their evening just took a vital turn. "Let's go!" he said. As they drove the winding country roads, Frank filled Addie in on the details of the assault. "We have an eight-year-old female; she was brought in by paramedics. Mom arrived home and walked into the living room and saw her boyfriend on top of the child. He had the child on the floor, her PJs partially removed after he ripped them off. He was naked and on top of the child with his two hands around her small neck, strangling her. From what Mom told police officers at the scene, her daughter was lifeless and unconscious and her boyfriend was in a fixed trance, he didn't even know that she had come home. Mom grabbed an object. We're not sure what the object was, but hit 'boyfriend' in the back of his head, causing a pretty big wound. Patrol said there was a lot of blood in the living room from his head injury. The 'boyfriend' is in custody, and will go to jail after his head is stapled back together."

Addie listened intently to the somber details Frank was relaying, while he was driving on the two-lane country road. She was thinking of where the best forensic evidence would most likely be found on the child's body, pondering what she should collect first. "I will collect her PJs. I'll do ALS. I'll swab her mouth, chest, neck, genitals, legs. Oh! We have new teddy bears; I'll grab a teddy bear before I go in to see her. She can hold her teddy bear while I do her exam. I hope I don't cry. I could just burst into tears right now. Who could do such evil acts on a child? I wonder if she will still be alive by the time we arrive? The strangulation sounded pretty severe."

While thinking of the details, they crested the top of a hill. The thoughts about the young patient were interrupted...

Addie was awed by the grandeur of the moon rising from the dark horizon, beauty of such magnificence! The night sky, in a rare shade of satin sapphire brilliance, was offset by a prodigious orange moon, balancing on the horizon, so large and round; it appeared that you could easily reach out to touch it. The dichotomy of hurrying to a brutal crime in the presence of such majesty struck her. Tears slowly began to fill, as she blinked her tears down, to stop them from flowing. Frank uttered the last vile detail. Addie sighed and quietly commented, "Among all the evil, it *is* a wonderful world. It is wonderful because victims have 'us'. Those of 'us' who are committed to seeking justice and mercy in the face of unspeakable crimes."

THE END

Authors' Note

According to the FBI, "Rape is penetration, no matter how slight, of the vagina or anus with a body part or object or oral penetration by a sex organ of another person without the consent of the victim."

Over the last two decades forensic nurse examiners (FNE), have expanded their knowledge through advanced training in domestic violence, strangulation, gunshot wounds, neurobiology of trauma, forensic experiential interview techniques, and human trafficking.

The events in *Toluidine Blue* are based on the authors' combined 44 years of nursing experience in emergency, trauma, forensic nursing and death investigation. Even though names and crime scene locations are fictional, all of the forensic information is accurate. One of the authors also worked over 10 years as a death investigator.

Acknowledgments

From Evelyne Keating:

Thank you, Cousin Mary, for being my inspiration to write *Toluidine Blue*. Mary, I loved meeting you in Ocean City, MD, during the cold winter months to discuss the details of one day writing a novel. Sipping wine, marveling at the idea of creating characters based on real life forensic nurses. Thank you, my cousin Thomas Mulgrew III, for designing the cover of *Toluidine Blue*. You exceeded our expectations.

Roxanne "Rachel" Shoenfeld, thank you for being such a great friend and a wonderful death investigator and forensic nurse. Writing a novel with you has truly been a wonderful experience.

Sergeant Rose Moran's input is based on more than 40 years as a police officer. Her last 30 years as a Detective Sergeant in Homicide and the Special Victims Unit. Rose, a sincere Thank You in gratitude from Rox and I, as a contributor on the law enforcement perspective. Rose, you are not only a colleague, whom we have worked many cases with, but a dear friend as well. Sergeant Moran's favorite quote, when referring to the most egregious crimes, is: "Oh what a tangled web we weave when first we practice to deceive." (Sir Walter Scott)

To our boss, Laura, the manager of the sexual assault forensics unit. You set the stage for the immense level of loyalty, and support my fellow forensic nurses have for one another, by being loyal and supportive yourself.

Thank you to my husband 'Dr. Emory' and my daughters, Loren and Margaux for listening to my endless thoughts. You never faltered in your support. You kindly provided praise and the encouragement for me to continue. As for my mother Sally, it was fun discussing the book with you all for ideas. Thank you for helping with the final editing.

Lorie, my dear friend, thank you for editing the manuscript. Your input and suggestions were greatly appreciated throughout the novel. Thank you for your encouragement in writing *Toluidine Blue*.

Uncle Milt, Aunt Mary and Aunt Margaret thank you for your guidance, encouragement and suggestions. All of your input was valuable and it was wonderful to be able to call on family for support. Thank you! E.

From Roxanne Shoenfeld:

Thank you to my husband and to my mother-in-law for encouraging me to write and for their patience and support along the journey. I would also like to thank all of the first responders, both Fire Department and Police Department, whom I have worked with throughout my career. I have the deepest respect and appreciation for what you do. I would like to dedicate this to my daughter. Rachel, always remember you can achieve anything you set your mind to do, you just have to want it bad enough. I love you to the moon and back. R.

Sources

Banks, Duren, and Tracey Kyckelhahn. "Characteristics of Suspected Human Trafficking Incidents 2008-2010." Department of Justice, Apr. 2011, www.bjs.gov/content/pub/pdf/cshti0810.pdf.

Cassey, Ron. "Children of the Night: Sex Trafficking is Maryland's Dirty Open Secret." *Baltimore*, Mar. 2017, www.baltimoremagazine.com/2017/2/8/sex-trafficking-is-maryland-dirty-open-secret.

"Crime in the United States 2013 Rape." FBI-UCR, 2013, ucr.fbi.gov/crime-in-the-u.s/2013/crime-in-the-u.s.-2013/violent-crime/rape. Accessed 2018.

Effective Victim Interviewing Webinar. 2012. EVAWI, www.evawintl.org/WebinarDetail.aspx?webinarid=1012. Accessed Oct. 2017.
EVAWI.
www.evawintl.org//images/uploads/Forensic%20Compliance/Training%20Materials/Hopper%20-%20EVAWI%20Webinar%20-%20Sept%202016%20-%20Part%201%20-%20Handouts.pdf.

Forensic Experiential Trauma Interview: A Trauma Informed Experience 2-Part Webinar Series. Narrated by Jim Hopper, Dr, 2016. *EVAWI,*
www.evawintl.org/WebinarDetail.aspx?webinarid=1036. Accessed Oct. 2017.

Forensic Experiential Trauma Interview: A Trauma Informed Experience 2-Part Webinar Series. *EVAWI,*
www.evawintl.org/WebinarDetail.aspx?webinarid=1037.

"Forensic Medicine for Medical Students: Bitemarks." *Forensic Med.co.UK*, www.forensicmed.co.uk/wounds/bitemarks/.

"Human trafficking, Sex Trafficking, Recognizing the signs." *Polaris Freedom Happens Now*, polarisproject.org/human-trafficking/sex-trafficking.

Kaushal, N. "Human Bite Marks In Skin: A Review." *The Internet Journal of Biological Anthropology. 2010 Volume 4 Number 2.* ispub.com/IJBA/4/2/7763.

Locard, Dr. Edmond. *Forensic Handbook*, 12 Aug. 2012, www.forensichandbook.com/. Accessed Jan. 2018.

McCain, Cindy, and Malika Saada Saar. "Experts:Ohio Among Worst for Sex Trafficking." Cincinnati.com, *The Enquirer*, 22 Sept. 2015, www.cincinnati.com/story/opinion/contributors/2015/09/22/experts-ohio-among-worst-sex-trafficking/72613268/.

National Human Trafficking Hotline. humantraffickinghotline.org/type-trafficking/human-trafficking. Accessed 27 June 2018.

Neurobiology of trauma. Narrated by Jim Hopper, Dr. EVAWI. Accessed 2016.

Quigley, Anne. "There is a Longing In Our Hearts- lyrics." music match.com, www.musixmatch.com/lyrics/Anne-Quigley/There-Is-a-Longing.

Reading Victims and Judging Credibility. www.evawintl.org/WebinarDetail.aspx?webinarid=1046. Accessed Oct. 2017.

"Reading" Victims & Judging Credibility - Best Practices in Promoting Victim Centered Investigations & Prosecutions Webinar. 2017. *EVAWI*, www.evawintl.org/WebinarDetail.aspx?webinarid=1046.

Schreyer, Natalie. "Domestic abusers: Dangerous for women — and lethal for cops." *USA Today*, 9 Apr. 2018, www.usatoday.com/story/news/nation/2018/04/09/domestic-abusers-dangerous-women-and-lethal-cops/479241002/.

Sexual assault a trauma informed approach. NSVRC, www.michiganprosecutor.org/component/yendifvideoshare/video/9-trama-informed-approach-part-1.

Sexual assault a trauma informed approach. NSVRC, www.michiganprosecutor.org/component/yendifvideoshare/video/11-trama-informed-approach-part-2.

Smock, Bill, Dr. "Forensic Evaluation of Gunshot Wounds." International Association of Forensic Nurses Conference 2014, Oct. 2014, Phoenix, Arizona. Lecture.
---. "Forensic Evaluation of Gunshot Wounds Online Course." Galen Center for professional development, June 2015. Lecture. 24 Credits.

STAFF, SHI. "Why Her? What You Need To Know About How Pimps Choose." *Shared Hope*, 10 Apr. 2013, sharedhope.org/2013/04/why-her-what-you-need-to-know-about-how-pimps-choose/.
Understanding the neurobiology of trauma document library handler. www.evawintl.org/Library/DocumentLibraryHandler.ashx?id=842.

"What is Sex Trafficking?" *Shared Hope*, sharedhope.org/the-problem/what-is-sex-trafficking/. Accessed 27 June 2018.

About the Authors

Evelyne Keating is currently working as a forensic nurse examiner in Maryland. She graduated from Villa Julie College with a Bachelors of Science in nursing. She began her nursing career, 24 years ago, at a Level 1 Trauma Center, but most of her nursing career was spent working the night shift in a Baltimore city emergency room. She volunteered for several years as an EMT with a local Volunteer Fire Department. Currently, Evelyne is certified as a pediatric and adolescent/adult forensic nurse examiner (FNE) and holds the national level of certification through the International Association of Forensic Nurses. She has been working as a forensic nurse examiner for the last seven years of her nursing career. She teaches forensic evaluation of gunshot wounds, forensic experiential trauma techniques (FETI), forensic photography and injury interpretation. She was awarded "Baltimore's Best Nurse" in women's health. She has trained a service dog, named Maggie, for an honorably discharged wounded soldier. Evelyne is currently working with her German shepherd puppy Violet, hopefully she will become a therapy dog; providing comfort for victims and a reprieve for the nurses. She is married to a wonderful man, who supports all of her endeavors, and has two beautiful daughters and five pets.

Roxanne Shoenfeld graduated from the University of Maryland School of Nursing. She has nineteen years of nursing experience, including two in the Intensive Care Unit and fourteen in the Emergency Department. Currently, Roxanne is certified as a pediatric, adolescent and adult forensic nurse examiner, and has been working in that capacity for the past five years. She also worked as a Forensic Investigator for the Office of the Chief Medical Examiner for nine years, performing death investigation in Maryland. Roxanne worked with a hospital-based Domestic Violence program for 7 years, working on the Strangulation Response Project, the Forensic Light Source Project, taking call for the Lethality Line and assisting in the training of Physicians, Nurses and Emergency Medical Service Providers in domestic violence related topics She is on the Steering Committee of the Maryland Healthcare Coalition Against Domestic Violence and is a member at large on the Baltimore County Domestic Violence Fatality Review Board. Roxanne attended the National Institute for Strangulation Training and

Prevention in San Diego in 2013 and the Master's level Strangulation Course in August, 2018. She educates judges, prosecutors, police, medical personnel, advocates and first responders in the fire department in Maryland on the topic of non-fatal strangulation. She has been married to her husband for 37 years. She has a wonderful daughter and a cat named Reanna.

CPSIA information can be obtained
at www.ICGtesting.com
Printed in the USA
LVHW111737190319
611165LV00002B/207/P

9 781796 904543